DISCARD

THE REAL
RIO D'AQUILA

THE REAL RIO D'AQUILA

BY

SANDRA MARTON

First published in Great Britain 2011
by Mills & Boon, an imprint of Harlequin (UK) Limited.
Large Print edition 2012
Harlequin (UK) Limited, Eton House,
18-24 Paradise Road, Richmond, Surrey TW9 1SR

© Sandra Marton 2011

ISBN: 978 0 263 22559 4

Harlequin (UK) policy is to use papers that are natural, renewable and recyclable products and made from wood grown in sustainable forests. The logging and manufacturing process conform to the legal environmental regulations of the country of origin.

Printed and bound in Great Britain
by CPI Antony Rowe, Chippenham, Wiltshire

CHAPTER ONE

Rio D'Aquila was known for many things.

He was wealthy beyond most people's measure, feared by those who had reason to fear him and as ruggedly good-looking as any man could hope to be.

Not that Rio gave a damn about his looks.

Who he was or, rather, who he had become, was what mattered.

He had been born to poverty, not in Brazil, despite his name, but on the meanest possible streets of Naples, Italy.

At seventeen, he'd stowed away on a rusting Brazilian freighter. The crew had dubbed him "Rio" because that was the ship's destination; they'd tagged on the "Aquila" because he'd responded with the fierceness of an eagle to their taunting.

The name had suited him much more than Matteo Rossi, which was what the sisters at the orphanage where he'd been raised had called him. "Rossi" was pretty much the Italian equivalent of "Smith." "Matteo," they'd said with gentle piety, meant a gift from God.

Rio had always known he was hardly that, so he took the name Rio D'Aquila and made it his own.

He was thirty-two now, and the boy he'd been was a distant memory.

Rio inhabited a world in which money and power were the lingua franca, and often as not handed down as an absolute right from father to son.

Rio's father, or maybe his mother, had given him nothing but midnight-black hair, dark blue eyes, a handsome if rugged face and a leanly muscled, six-foot-three-inch body.

Everything else he owned—the homes, the cars, the planes, the corporate giant known as Eagle Enterprises—he had acquired for himself.

There was nothing wrong with that. Starting life without any baggage, getting to the top on your own, was all the sweeter. If there was one drawback, it was that his kind of success attracted attention.

At first, he'd enjoyed it. Picking up the *Times* in the morning, seeing his name or his photo in the financial section had made him feel, well, successful.

Inevitably, he'd not only wearied of it, he'd realized how meaningless it was.

The simple truth was that a man who ranked in the top ten on the *Forbes* list made news just by existing. And when that man was a bachelor inevitably described as "eligible," meaning he had not yet been snared by some calculating female who wanted his name, his status and his money…

When that happened, a man lost all privacy.

Rio valued his privacy as much as he despised being a topic of conversation.

Not that Rio cared much what people said, whether it was that he was brilliant and tough. Or brilliant and heartless. He was who he was, and all that mattered was his adherence to his own code of ethics.

He believed in honesty, determination, intensity of focus, logic—and emotional control. Emotional control was everything.

Still, on this hot August afternoon, cicadas droning in the fields behind him, the hiss of the surf beating against the shore, he was ready to admit that logic and control were fast slipping from his grasp.

He was, to put it bluntly, angry as hell.

In Manhattan, when a business deal drove him to the point of rage, he headed for his gym and the ring in its center for a couple of rounds with a sparring partner, but he wasn't in New York. He was as far east of the city as a man could get without putting his feet in the Atlantic.

He was in the town of Southampton, on Long Island's exclusive South Shore. He was here in search of that increasingly elusive thing called privacy and, goddamnit, he was not going to let some fool named Izzy Orsini spoil the day for him.

For the past hour, Rio had taken his temper out on a shovel.

If any of his business associates could have seen him now, they'd have been stunned. Rio D'Aquila, dressed in jeans, a T-shirt and work boots? Rio D'Aquila, standing in a trench and shoveling dirt?

Impossible.

But Rio had dug ditches before, not that anyone in his world knew it. And though he sure as hell hadn't expected to be doing any digging today, it was better than standing around and getting more ticked off by the minute.

Especially when, until a couple of hours ago, he'd had a damned good day.

He'd flown in early, piloting his own plane to the small airport at Easthampton where he'd picked up the black Chevy Silverado his property manager had left for him. Then he'd driven the short distance to Southampton.

The town was small, picturesque and quiet early on a Friday morning. Rio had parked, gone into a small café where he'd had breakfast with the guy who was putting in the infinity pool at the house he'd recently had built. The pool would extend over the dunes from the second floor terrace, and they'd talked about its size and the view he'd have. The conversation had been pleasant, almost as pleasant as being able to sit in a restaurant without being the unwilling center of attention.

That was part of the reason he'd decided to build a weekend home here, on six outrageously expensive acres of land that overlooked the ocean.

For the most part—and there were always exceptions to the rule, of course—nobody bothered celebrities in these small eastern Long Island villages. And Rio, God help him, was a celebrity, according to the crazy media.

Here, he could be himself. Have a meal. Take a walk. It was like an unwritten code. Build here, become, for the most part, invisible.

For a man who sometimes had to travel with a phalanx of bodyguards or with a limo crawling along at the curb so he could duck into it, fast, and be whisked away, it was a minor miracle.

So Rio had enjoyed his bacon and eggs, strolled the streets for a while, even checked the hardware store as if he really were going to need to buy hammers and saws.

In fact, there'd been a time he'd owned such tools and used them to earn his daily bread. A little wistfully, he thought about maybe putting in some shelves in his new house, if he could find a place in it that needed them. He wasn't foolish enough to believe that working with your hands gave you special moral status but there was something to be said about leading a simpler life.

At midmorning, he met with the security specialist who'd installed an ultrasophisticated system in and around the house. They sat at a table on the flagstone patio of a little ice cream shop, the sun blocked by a big blue umbrella.

Rio tried to remember the last time he'd had a strawberry ice cream sundae and couldn't.

He felt…what? Lazy. Content. He almost had to force himself to pay attention to the conversation.

There was a malfunction of the security system at the gate. The intercom wasn't working right. His caretaker had told him voices coming over the intercom were almost indecipherably drowned in static, and the gate's locking mechanism didn't always work.

The area was pleasant, there was nothing but a discreet plaque on the gate that said Eagle's Nest, but Rio wasn't a fool. A man like him needed security.

"Not to worry," the security guy assured him. "I'll come out Monday morning and deal with it, first thing."

At noon, Rio had driven to his house. The long driveway had not yet been finished and the tires bounced along over small stones and deep ruts but nothing could dim the pleasure he already took in the place.

The house was just as he'd wanted it. Light

wood. Lots of glass. It would be his retreat from the dog-eat-dog world he inhabited 24/7.

The guy he'd hired as his contractor was waiting. They had some things to discuss, nothing major, and then, together, they'd interview three applicants for the job of landscaping the rear terrace and two decks.

No. Not three applicants. Four. Damned if he didn't keep forgetting that. Rio had some definite ideas about what he wanted. Whomever he hired would have to understand that he'd be an active participant in the plans he drew up, just as he'd been an active participant in the design of the house.

The caretaker was there, too, but just leaving. He told Rio he'd taken the liberty of filling the freezer and fridge with a few things.

"Breakfast stuff. You know, eggs, bacon, bread. And steaks, some local corn and tomatoes, even a couple of bottles of wine. Just in case you decide to spend the night."

Rio thanked him, though he had no plans to spend the night. As it was, he'd canceled a couple of meetings so he could get here but it had turned out to be the only chance for all three landscaping candidates to show up for interviews on the same day.

Four. Four candidates. How come he couldn't keep that in his head?

Probably because he wasn't hot on interviewing that fourth one, he thought, and gave a mental sigh. It was never a good idea to mix friendship and business, but when one of your pals asked you to at least talk to his cousin or uncle, or whatever in hell somebody named Izzy Orsini was to Dante Orsini, well, you bent the rules and did it.

After a few minutes, Rio took a picnic hamper from the Silverado's cab. His housekeeper in Manhattan had packed lunch at his request. It turned out to be an elegant one. Thinly sliced cold roast beef on French baguettes, a chunk of properly aged Vermont cheddar, a bottle of chilled *prosecco,* fresh strawberries and tiny butter pastries.

Plus, of course, linen napkins, stemware and china mugs.

Rio and the contractor grinned at each other. They were both wearing jeans, sitting on a pair of overturned buckets on the unfinished terrace, their meal arranged on a plank laid over a sawhorse.

Cold beer and a couple of ham and cheese on rye might have been more in keeping with things, but the lunch was good and they finished every mouthful.

The landscapers started arriving not long after that. They showed up one at a time, exactly as scheduled, Rio buzzing them in through the gate, which seemed to be working perfectly. They were local men, each efficient and businesslike and politely eager to win what would be a substantial contract.

All of them came equipped with glossy folders filled with computerized designs, suggested layouts, sketches, photos of prior projects and spreadsheets of mind-numbing detail.

Each listened carefully as Rio explained what they already knew. He wanted the perimeter of the terrace planted in as natural a manner as possible. The decks, as well. Greenery. Shrubs. Flowers, maybe. Or flowering shrubs. Rio was willing to admit what he knew about gardening could fit into a teaspoon with room left over, but he made it clear that he knew the overall effect he was going for.

"What I want," he told each applicant, "is to

have the terrace seem to flow out of the fields behind the house. Does that make sense to you?"

Each man nodded earnestly; each roughed out some quick ideas on a sketchpad and though none of the sketches had been exactly what Rio intended, he'd known instantly that he could choose any of the three guys and, ultimately, be satisfied.

Three excellent landscapers.

But, of course, there was a fourth.

The contractor said he understood. A friend of a friend. He knew how that was. The friend of a friend was late but the two men settled in to wait.

And wait.

After a while, Rio frowned.

"The guy should know better than to be late," he said.

The contractor agreed. "Maybe he had a flat. Or something."

"Or something," Rio said.

Another ten minutes went by. Damnit, Rio thought, if only he hadn't gone to that party, he wouldn't be waiting to interview another landscaper at all.

The party had taken place a few weeks ago. Dante Orsini and his wife, Gabriella, had invited some people to their penthouse for a charity bash. Rio had gone with a date, a woman he'd been seeing for a couple of months.

She went off to the powder room.

The "little girls' room" she'd called it, and Dante had rolled his eyes at Rio, put a drink in his hand and led him out to the terrace, where it was quieter and less crowded.

"The little girls' room, huh?"

Rio had grinned. "All good things come to an end," he'd answered, and Dante had grinned, too, because he still remembered his bachelor days.

The friends had touched glasses, drunk some of their bourbon. Then, Dante had cleared his throat.

"So, we hear you're building a place in the Hamptons."

Rio had nodded. Word got around. Nothing new to that. New York was a big city but people like he and Dante moved in relatively small circles.

"Southampton," he'd said. "I visited a friend there one weekend last summer. Lucas Viera. You know him? Anyway, Viera has a house on the beach. Very private, very quiet. I liked what I saw, and now—"

"And now," Gabriella Orsini had said, smiling as she joined the men and slipped her arm through her husband's, "you need a landscaper." Her smile broadened. "You do, don't you?"

Rio had shrugged. "Well, sure, but—"

"We just happen to know a very good one."

To Rio's amazement, Dante had blushed.

"Izzy," Gabriella had said. She'd nodded toward the lush plantings along the borders of the terrace. "That's Izzy's work. Spectacular, don't you think?"

Rio had looked at the plantings. Not spectacular, but nice. Natural-looking, which could not have been easy to accomplish when the setting was a three-level penthouse in the sky.

"Uh," Dante had said, "see, Izzy is sort of trying to branch out, and—"

"And," Gabriella had said sweetly, "we're not above a bit of nepotism. Are we, darling?"

The penny had finally dropped.

His friend, actually, his friend's wife, was hustling the work of one of her husband's relatives. A cousin, maybe an uncle, because there were only four Orsini brothers. Rio had met them all and not one was named Izzy.

Whatever, it didn't matter.

The terrace plantings had looked good. And, what the hell, Rio liked Dante and Gabriella, who happened to have been born in Brazil, his adopted country. So when it came time to deal with the landscaping, Rio gave Izzy Orsini's name and email address to his contractor, who'd made the contact and set up the time and date of the meeting.

A meeting for which Izzy Orsini had not showed.

Time had passed, with the contractor trying hard not to look at his watch until, finally, Rio had thought, *basta.* Enough. He'd told the contractor he was free to leave.

"I'm sure you have better things to do than wait around for some guy who's going to be a no-show."

"You sure, Mr. D'Aquila? 'Cause if you want, I can—"

"It's Rio, remember? And it's not a problem. I'll hang around for a while, just in case."

Which, Rio thought grimly as he dug the shovel into the soil in the trench, brought things straight to the present.

To two bloody hours, waiting for Izzy Orsini to put in an appearance.

"Merda," he muttered, and stabbed the shovel blade into the earth again.

His temper was rising in inverse proportion to the depth of the trench which would ultimately be the foundation for a low stone wall but at the rate he was going, he was liable to dig his way to China.

He'd run out of excuses for Dante's cousin.

Rio leaned on the shovel handle, wiped sweat from his eyes with a tightly muscled forearm.

Maybe Orsini got the time wrong. Maybe he'd had a flat. Maybe his great-aunt had come down with an attack of ague, or whatever it was great-aunts came down with, assuming he had a great-aunt at all.

Any of those things could have been explained by a phone call, but Orsini had not called.

Rio's lips thinned.

Okay. He'd wasted enough time on this. It would be sticky, telling Dante and Gabriella what had happened, but he'd had it.

A shadow passed overhead. Rio looked up, tilted his head back, watched a squadron of pelicans soar overhead, aiming for the ocean. The cool, refreshing ocean.

That did it.

He yanked the shovel free of the soil and put it back where he'd found it.

He'd bought this place as somewhere he could relax. Well, he damned well wasn't relaxing now. Thinking about an idiot who'd let a chance at a job like this slip through his fingers made his blood boil.

Back when he was just starting out, he'd never have let something so important get away. He'd have walked, crawled, done whatever it took to snag even a chance at a job that would pay well and could lead to something even better.

No wonder Gabriella was hustling this Orsini jerk. The fool couldn't do anything on his own.

Rio stretched and rotated his shoulders. His muscles ached. He'd skinned a couple of knuckles and there was dirt under his usually well-manicured fingernails.

The truth was, he'd enjoyed a couple of hours of work. Real work, physical work just as he enjoyed being in the ring at his gym. But enough was enough.

Sweat dripped off the end of his nose. He yanked his T-shirt over his head and used it to mop his face.

The sun was starting to drop lower in the sky. The day was coming to an end. He hated to leave. The city would be hot and noisy...

Rio made a quick decision.

He'd take that swim. Then, instead of flying back to Manhattan, he'd spend the night here. Hell, why not? Most of the furniture he'd ordered was in. Thanks to his property manager, he had steaks, fresh corn, even wine. The more he thought about it, the better it—

Bzzzz.

What the hell was that? A bee? A wasp? No. It was the intercom at the gate.

He wasn't expecting anyone...

Bzzzz. Bzzzz. Bzzzz.

Orsini. It had to be. The fool had shown up after all, except he was three hours late.

Rio almost laughed. The guy had *cojones,* he had to give him that, but that was all he had. No way was he going to buzz him in. The business of the day was over. This was his own time. His quiet time. His—

Bzzzz. Bzzzz. Bzzzz. Bzzzz.

Rio folded his arms. Stood his ground.

The damned thing buzzed again.

Cristo! What would it take to get rid of the guy?

More buzzing. Rio narrowed his eyes, marched to the intercom and depressed the button.

"What?" he snarled.

A blast of static roared from the speaker.

Rio cursed, slapped the button. No good. Orsini had to be leaning on the button at his end, or maybe the freaking thing wasn't working again. Nothing but static was coming through.

Bzzzz. Bzzzz. Bzzzz. Bzzzz.

His jaw tightened. If Orsini wanted in, then "in" and a lesson on courtesy and punctuality was what he'd get. And he was in the mood to give it to him.

Rio balled up his T-shirt and tossed it aside, yanked open the glass French doors that led into the great room, marched through the house to the entry foyer, his work boots leaving muddy prints on the Carrara marble floors.

"Damnit," he roared, as he flung open the front door—

And stopped.

A figure was coming toward him, hurrying up

the long, unfinished driveway. Trying to hurry, at any rate, but how fast could a person go on that uneven, pitted, rocky surface in—in—

Were those stiletto heels?

His visitor was not Izzy Orsini.

It was a woman.

Damn the malfunctioning intercom and gate!

He'd been this route one time before. A woman had decided he was her true love. He'd never talked to her, never heard her name, never seen her in his life but he'd turned out to be a fixture in her mental landscape. She'd sent him letters. Emails. She'd sent him gifts and cards. She'd stalked him without letup, settled in on the corner near his Manhattan condo, which was when he'd finally, if reluctantly, pressed charges.

Was this her again?

No. His stalker had been fiftyish, short and rotund. This woman was young. Mid-twenties. Tall and slender, and dressed as if she were on her way to a board meeting: the stilettos, a white blouse showing under the suit jacket, dark hair pulled severely back from her face. She didn't look like a crazy stalker or like a nosy reporter, though in Rio's book, the two could easily be one and the same, but who gave a damn?

She had no business here and that was all that mattered.

"Hold it right there," Rio barked, but his command didn't stop her and he trotted down the steps, eyes narrowed. "I said—"

"Mr. D'Aquila expects me."

Not a reporter or a crazy, at least not one looking for him if she didn't recognize him, even shirtless, in jeans and work boots, but clearly a liar with an agenda all her own.

Rio gave a thin smile.

"I assure you, madam, that would be news to him."

There were only a couple of feet between them now. Close up, he could see that there was a rip in her skirt, dirt on those stiletto heels and a smudge on her blouse. Her hair wasn't quite as neatly drawn back as he'd at first thought; tendrils of it, dark and curling, were coming loose around her face.

It was an interesting face. Triangular. High cheekbones. Big green eyes. Feline, he thought.

Not that it mattered, but if she'd been in some kind of accident he supposed he could, at least, offer to—

* * *

"It is your attitude that would be news to him," Isabella Orsini said, hoping her voice would not tremble because everything inside her was bouncing around like an unset bowl of gelatin and after all she'd gone through today, there wasn't a way in hell she was going to permit this half-naked, good-looking-if-you-were-foolish-enough-to-like-the-type flunky of a too rich, too powerful, too full-of-himself ape to stop her now.

There was a moment's silence. Then Mr. Half-Naked raised one dark eyebrow.

"Really."

His tone was soft but it made Izzy's heart thump. To hell with thumping hearts, she thought, and lifted her chin.

"Really," she said, with all the hauteur she could muster.

Mr. Half-Naked gave another of those thin smiles and motioned toward the door.

"In that case," he said, in a voice that was almost a purr, "you had better come in."

CHAPTER TWO

A NAKED man.

A house in the middle of nowhere.

An open door, and an invitation to step through it.

Izzy swallowed hard.

Did she truly want to do that? She was not into taking risks. Everyone knew that about her, even her father, who didn't actually know anything about any of his children.

I have heard that you are considering taking on a new client, Isabella, Cesare Orsini had said during one of the inevitable Sunday command performance dinners at the Orsini mansion. *But you will not.*

"Excuse me?" Izzy had said.

Her father had given her what she'd always thought of as one of his "I am the head of this family" glares except, of course, his glares as *don* of the East Coast's most powerful *famiglia* had more impact on those who feared him than they did on his sons and daughters.

To them, he was not the head of anything. He was just a shame to be borne for the sake of their mother.

"Do I not speak English as well as you? I said, you are not to work for Rio D'Aquila."

"And you say this because…?"

"I know of him and I do not like what I know. Therefore, accepting a position that will make you his servant is out of the question."

Isabella would have laughed had her father's view of what she did for a living not been such an old argument.

"I am not a servant, Father, I am a horticulturist with a degree from the University of Connecticut."

"You are a gardener."

"I certainly am. And what if I were what you call a servant? There's nothing dishonorable in being a maid or a cook."

"Orsinis do not bow their heads or bend their knees to anyone, Isabella. Is that clear?"

Nothing had been clear, starting with how her father had learned she'd been invited to bid on a job for a billionaire she'd never even heard of until a couple of weeks ago, going straight through to how Cesare could have imagined she would take orders from him.

If anything, his certainty that she would click her heels and obey him was what had convinced her to give serious consideration to the offer, something she really had not intended until then.

Now here she was, in Southampton, a place that might as well have been Mars for all she knew about it, hours late for an important interview, her car in a ditch, her suit and her shoes absolute disasters.

No. She was not going to think about that now. It would be self-defeating…and hadn't she had enough of that?

It was enough to wonder at the crazed logic of moving past an all-but-naked man, a gorgeous all-but-naked man, to step inside a house that was, conservatively speaking, the size of an airplane hangar.

"Well? Are you coming inside, or have you changed your mind about Mr. D'Aquila expecting you?"

Izzy blinked. The caretaker, or whatever he was,

was watching her with amusement. Forget amusement. That expression on his face was a smirk.

How lovely to be the day's entertainment, Isabella thought, and drew herself to her full five foot seven.

"I am not in the habit of changing my mind about anything," she said, and almost winced.

Such a stupid thing to say.

Too late.

She'd said it and now her feet, which seemingly had only a tenuous connection to her brain, propelled her past him, up a set of wide steps, through a massive door and into the house. She jumped as the door slammed shut behind her.

She wanted to think it was with the sound of doom but the truth was, it was the sound of a door slamming, nothing more, nothing less…

And ohmygod, the entry foyer was so big! It was huge!

"Yes. It is, isn't it?"

She spun around. Mr. Half-Naked was standing right in back of her, arms folded across his chest. A very impressive chest, all muscle and golden skin and dark curls.

Her gaze skimmed lower.

A six-pack, she thought, sucking in her breath. Those bands of muscle really did exist, neatly bisected by silky-looking hair that arrowed down and down and…

"The foyer," he said, his voice not just amused but smoky. Her gaze flew to his. "You were thinking it was big. Huge, in fact." A smile tilted the corner of his lips. "That was what you were referring to, wasn't it?"

She felt her face heat. Had she spoken aloud? She must have, but she'd certainly never meant to infer…

Isabella narrowed her eyes. Damn the man!

He was playing games at her expense.

Still, she could hardly blame him.

He might be only half-dressed but she—

She was a mess.

Everything she had on was stained, torn or smudged. A few hours ago, she'd looked perfect. Well, as perfect as she could ever look. She'd taken more time preparing for this meeting than she'd ever prepared for anything in her life.

Actually, she hadn't done a thing.

Anna had done it all.

A suit instead of her usual jeans. A wool suit,

hot as blazes on a day like this but, Anna had said, The Proper Thing for such an important interview. A silk blouse instead of a T-shirt. Shoes rather than sandals, and with heels so ridiculously high she could hardly walk in them, especially the million miles she'd had to plod after that rabbit had somehow materialized in the middle of the road and her car had taken a nosedive into that miserable ditch.

All of it was Anna's, of course. The suit, the blouse, the shoes.

The car.

Oh, God, the car!

Forget that for now.

She had to concentrate on what lay ahead, the all-important chance to transform Growing Wild from a shoe-box operation in a cheap storefront on what was most definitely not a trendy street near the Gowanus Canal to an elegant shop—an elegant *shoppe,* Anna had joked—in SoHo. Or in the Village. Or on the Upper East Side.

No.

She'd never go that far.

The truth was, she liked the neighborhood she was in, seedy as it was, but she had to admit the growth of her little landscaping business was dependent on location and on landing a couple of really important clients. Aside from the admitted pleasure of defying her father, that was why she'd agreed to the interview with Rio D'Aquila, a man the papers called a removed, cold, heartless multibillionaire.

Heaven knew she was familiar enough with the type.

Izzy's work was skilled and imaginative; she used only the most beautiful flowers and greenery. That made her services costly. It made them the province of the very rich.

And dealing with them was sometimes unpleasant. It was sometimes downright horrible. The very rich could be totally self-serving, completely selfish, uncaring of others...

"They're not all like that," Anna had said.

Well, no. Her brothers were very rich. So was Anna's husband. But—

"But," Anna had said, with incontrovertible logic, "if you're going to have to like a person before you take him as a client, Isabella, you're never going to make Growing Wild a success."

True enough. And when you coupled that simple

wisdom with the fact that the offer was important enough for Anna to refer to her as Isabella…

Well, that had convinced her.

Unfortunately, Izzy was here, not Anna.

Sophisticated Anna would have known how to handle the situation. She would not have gotten lost or crashed the car. She certainly would not have turned up hours late for this appointment.

And she absolutely would not have let a man like this intimidate her. She'd have known how to handle the half-dressed muscleman who was having such fun at her expense.

That smirk was still on his face.

It infuriated her. After the day she'd had, Izzy was in no mood to be laughed at, certainly not by him.

She knew his type.

Good-looking. Glib-tongued. Full of himself, especially when it came to women, because women, the silly fools, undoubtedly threw themselves at his feet with all the grace of—of salmon throwing themselves upstream.

Okay, a bad metaphor. The point was, she was not a woman to be intimidated by an empty-headed stud. She was a self-sufficient businesswoman, never mind that she wasn't self-sufficient enough to be wearing her own clothes or driving her own car.

All that mattered was that she was here. And time was wasting. The sun would set soon, and then what?

Then what, indeed?

The caretaker was leaning against a table, hands tucked into the back pockets of his jeans. She had a choice of views. His incredible face. His incredible chest. The tight fit of those faded jeans—

Stop it, she told herself sternly, and set her gaze squarely on his chin.

"Look," she said, "I really don't have time for this."

"For what?"

Was the man dense?

"Where is your boss?"

That won her a shrug. "He's around."

The answer, the lazy lift of those shoulders, those amazingly broad shoulders, infuriated her. All that macho. That attitude. That testosterone.

That naked chest.

Damnit, she was back to that and it was his fault. She'd have bet it was deliberate.

Izzy narrowed her eyes.

"Do you think you could possibly muster up enough ambition to find him and tell him I'm here?"

Mr. Half-Naked didn't move. Not a muscle. Well, that wasn't true. He did move a muscle; one corner of his mouth lifted, either in question or in another bout of hilarity at her expense.

Could you actually feel your blood pressure rising?

"One problem," he said lazily. "I'm still waiting for you to tell me why you're here."

The simplest thing would be to do exactly that. Just say, *I'm here to meet with Mr. D'Aquila and talk about landscaping this property.*

It was certainly not a secret.

The problem was, she didn't like Mr. All Brawn and No Brains's attitude.

Okay. That wasn't fair.

Just because he looked like he'd stepped off one of those calendars her roommate used to drool over in her college-dorm days didn't mean he was stupid.

It only meant he was so beautiful that looking at him made her heart do a little two-step, and that was surely ridiculous, almost as ridiculous as this silly power game they were playing.

Who cared if it was silly? She was entitled to win at something today!

"What are you?" she said sarcastically. "His appointment secretary?"

One dark eyebrow rose again. "Maybe I'm his butler."

She stared at him for a long minute. Then she laughed.

Rio grinned.

He was really getting to her. Good. Fine. It was a lot more rewarding to take his pent-up irritation out on the woman, whoever she was, than on a trench.

"His butler, huh?" Her chin went up. "One thing's for sure, mister. I guarantee you're going to be looking for another job two minutes after I meet your employer."

Rio folded his arms over his chest.

The lady was losing her temper. Let her lose it. Let her get ticked off. Let her see how it felt to be frustrated enough to want Izzy Orsini to finally show up if only so that he could deck the jerk. If that was unfair—

Hey, life was unfair. Besides, the lady wasn't exactly behaving like a lady.

Well, yeah, she was.

Her clothes were a mess, but they were expensive.

So was her attitude.

He was the peasant, she was the princess. Only one problem in that little scenario.

The princess had no idea he held all the cards.

Well, not quite all. He still didn't know what had brought her here. The only certainty was that her presence could not possibly have anything to do with him.

Maybe she sold magazines door to door.

Maybe Southampton had designated her its Fruitcake of the Month.

Whoever she was, whatever she was, she was a welcome diversion. This little farce was fast becoming the best part of his long and irritating afternoon.

She was also very easy on the eyes, now that he'd had the chance to get a longer look at her.

The made-for-midwinter suit was rumpled, torn and a little dirty, but he was pretty sure it hid a made-for-midsummer-bikini body. Wool or no wool, he could make out the thrust of high breasts, the indentation of a feminine waist, the curve of rounded hips.

Rio frowned.

What the hell had put that into his head?

She was a woman, and women were not on his current agenda. He'd just ended an affair—women called them "relationships" but men knew better—and, as always, getting out of it had been a lot more difficult than getting in. Women were creatures of baffling complexity and despite what they all said, they inevitably ended up wanting something he could not, would not, give.

Commitment. Marriage.

Chains.

Rio moved fast. He intended to keep moving fast, to climb to the absolute top of every mountain that caught his interest. Why be handicapped by things he didn't want or need? Why anchor himself to one woman and inevitably tire of her?

He had to admit, though, some women were more intriguing than others.

This one, for instance.

She was tough. Or brave. Maybe that was the better word for her.

Standing up to him took courage at the best of times. Right now, looking as he did, half-naked, unkempt, hell, downright scruffy—he hadn't even shaved this morning, now that he thought about it—took *colhões*. Or *cojones*. The point was the same, in Portuguese or in Italian. Facing him down took courage. No, he didn't look like Jack the Ripper but he sure as hell didn't look like he'd stepped out of *GQ,* which was surely the kind of guy she normally dealt with.

This was, after all, the weekend haunt of the rich and famous. The I-Want-to-Be-Alone rich and famous, but that didn't change the fact that he wasn't usually the kind of guy who met you at the front door.

Given all that, he supposed you could call her foolish instead of brave. A woman who went toe-to-toe with a stranger, who walked into a house with a man she'd never seen before…

Foolish, sure.

But determined. Gutsy.

It was clear she wasn't going to give ground until she met Rio D'Aquila.

A gentleman would have made it easy. *I'm Rio D'Aquila,* a gentleman would have said, right up-front, or if he'd let things go on for a while, he'd smile at her now, apologize for any confusion and introduce himself.

A muscle flickered in Rio's jaw.

Yes, but he had not always been a gentleman. And right now, suddenly turning into one held no appeal.

The truth was, as soon as Rio D'Aquila appeared, all this would stop.

The bantering. The courage. Probably even the little blushes she tried to conceal each time she reminded herself that he wasn't wearing a shirt.

He liked it. All of it. He couldn't remember the last time he'd seen a woman blush, or the last time one had stood up to him.

It had been at least a decade on both counts, right around the time he'd made his first million.

The truth was, he was enjoying himself, playing at being someone he had once been. A man, not a name or a corporation or, even worse, a line in a gossip column.

Hell, there was nothing wrong with the game he was playing. It was just an extension of what had prompted him to buy the land and put up a house here in the first place.

He was being himself.

Rio frowned. And faced facts, because all that entire bit of justification was pure, unadulterated crap.

This was not who he was.

He didn't dig ditches. He didn't walk around half-dressed unless he was alone or unless he'd just been to bed with a woman, and what did that have to do with anything happening right now?

The point was, he was honest with people. Even with women, and that was occasionally difficult. No matter the situation, he never played games at a woman's expense.

It was just that this particular woman was a puzzle, and he had always liked puzzles.

Why was she dressed for winter when it was summer? Why was there a rip in her skirt, dirt on those come-and-get-me stilettos, a smudge on her blouse?

Now that he took a better look, there was a streak of dirt on her cheek, too.

It was an elegant cheek. Highly arched. Rose hued. And, he was certain, silken to the touch.

Her hair looked as if it would feel that way, too. It was dark. Lustrous. She'd yanked it back, secured it at the nape of her neck, but it refused to stay confined.

Tendrils were coming loose.

One in particular lay against her temple, daring him to reach for it, let it curl around his finger, see if it felt as soft as it looked.

She had great eyes. A nice nose. And she had a lovely mouth.

Pink. Generous but not, he was sure, pumped full of whatever horror it was that turned women into fish-lipped monstrosities.

One thing was certain.

Despite the classic suit, the demure blouse, the pulled back hair, that mouth was made for sin.

For sin, Rio thought, and felt his body stir.

Hell.

He swung away from her, irritated with himself for his unexpected reaction, with her for causing it. She was on his turf and she had no right to be there.

For a man who liked puzzles, the only one that needed solving was figuring out why he hadn't ended this charade before it began.

Truth time, Rio thought, and he unfolded his arms and took a long breath.

"Okay," he said, "enough."

His unwanted guest turned paper-white. *Cristo,* he thought, and cursed himself for being a fool.

"No," he said quickly, "I didn't mean…" He forced a smile. "There's nothing to be afraid of."

"I'm not afraid," she said, but, damnit, her voice was shaking.

"You don't understand." He went toward her, held out his hand. She stared at it. He did, too, saw the redness of his knuckles, the dirt on his skin and under his nails, drew his hand back and wiped it on his jeans. "I shouldn't have made things so difficult. You don't want to tell me who you are until you're positive Rio D'Aquila is here, that's fine."

"It doesn't matter," she said quickly. "I'll just— I'll just phone Mr. D'Aquila from the city—"

"Is that where you're from? New York?"

"Yes—but really, you don't have to—"

"Obviously," he said, trying to lighten things, "I'm not the butler."

He waited. After a few seconds, she gave him a hesitant smile.

"No," she said, "I didn't think you were."

Okay. It was time. He had the feeling she

was going to be furious at his subterfuge but it wouldn't matter.

He'd identify himself as the man she'd come to see, she'd tell him why she was here—something to do with town records, he'd bet, because it suddenly occurred to him that there'd been some sort of paper his lawyer had said he had to sign.

Whatever, they'd introduce themselves, he'd scribble his signature on the document she produced, and that would be the end of it.

"So," Rio said, "let's start from scratch."

He extended his hand again. She looked at it, at him, and then she put her hand in his. It was a small, feminine hand; his all but swallowed it and yet, he could feel calluses on her fingers, which surprised him.

The coolness of her skin surprised him, too. It was a warm day. Was she still nervous about him? It was definitely time to identify himself and set her concerns at ease.

"Hello," he said, and smiled. "I'm—"

"The handyman."

He almost laughed. "Well, no. Not exact—"

"The caretaker. Sorry." She swiped the tip of

her tongue over her lips, leaving them pink and delicately moist. "Nice to meet you"

"Yes." He dragged his gaze from her mouth. "And you are…?"

"Oh. Sorry. I'm the landscaper."

Maybe he hadn't heard her right. "Excuse me?"

"Well, not *the* landscaper. I'm an applicant." She looked around, then lowered her voice. "I'm late. Terribly late, but—"

"But?" he said carefully.

"But still, where's your boss? He was expecting me. You know, Isabella Orsini. From Growing Wild?"

"You?" Rio heard his voice rise. Hell, why not? He could feel his eyebrows shooting for his hairline. "You're Izzy Orsini?"

"That's me." She gave a nervous laugh. "And I hope this Rio D'Aquila isn't, you know, what I heard he was."

"What you heard he was?" he said, and wondered when in hell he'd turned into a parrot.

"Cold. Ruthless. Bad-tempered."

Rio cleared his throat. "Well, I suppose some people might say he was simply a—"

"An arrogant tyrant. But you don't have to like

someone to work for them, right? I mean, here you are, Mister—Mister—"

Rio didn't even hesitate.

"My name is Matteo," he said. "Matteo Rossi. And you have it right. I'm D'Aquila's caretaker."

CHAPTER THREE

MATTEO Rossi still had Izzy's hand trapped in his.

Well, no. Not trapped. Not exactly.

Just clasped, that was all. The pressure of his fingers over hers wasn't hard or unpleasant or threatening, it was simply—it was simply—

Masculine. Totally, completely, unquestionably masculine.

Everything about him was masculine, from the drop-dead-gorgeous face to the King-of-the-Centerfolds body, but then a man who did manual labor on an estate of this size wouldn't have to work up a sweat in a gym.

He was the real thing.

That was why those muscles in his shoulders, his biceps, his chest were so—so well-defined.

Isabella's mouth went dry.

Her interest, of course, was purely clinical. After all, she did manual labor, too. Planting, weeding, all those things, even when done on Manhattan terraces rather than Southampton estates, made for sweat and muscles. Combine that with what she recalled of college physiology and she could easily conjure up a mental image of him working, sweating…

Except, the images flashing through her head didn't have a damned thing to do with work. Not work done in a garden, anyway.

Actually, not anything a normal, healthy woman would call "work."

Or so she'd heard.

God, what was wrong with her? He was sweaty and good-looking. So what? Neither of those things had anything to do with sexual attraction…

Liar, she thought, and she pulled her hand free of his.

"For heaven's sake," she snapped, "don't you own a shirt?"

There was a moment of horrified silence. *No,* she thought, *please no, tell me I didn't say that…*

The caretaker made a choked sound. She jerked her head up, looked at him and, oh, Lord, he was trying not to laugh but his eyes met hers and a guffaw broke from his lips.

Isabella wanted to die. How could she have said such a thing?

Unfortunately, she knew the answer.

When it came to men, good-looking men, there were two Isabellas.

She met handsome men a lot. Her work took her into their homes; she accepted invitations to parties, even though she hated parties where you stood around nibbling on awful little canapés and gagging down overly sweet drinks with umbrellas stuck in them, because networking was the best way to find new clients.

Plus her brothers, gorgeous guys themselves, had recently taken to trying to find, with what they surely thought was subtlety, The Right Man for her.

"Hey," Dante or Rafe, Falco or Nick would say in the falsely cheerful giveaway tone she'd learned to recognize, "how about coming over for supper Friday evening?" Or Sunday brunch, or whatever was the latest excuse for introducing her to the latest candidate in the Orsini Brothers' "Let's Find a Guy for Izzy" plan.

To Isabella's chagrin, even Anna was getting into it, asking her to stop by and, surprise, surprise, a friend of Anna's handsome husband would just happen to stop by, too.

Hadn't any of them figured it out yet?

Put an attractive man in front of her and she either became tongue-tied or just the opposite, a woman whose mouth ran a hundred times faster than her brain.

Hi, a guy would say.

Her response? Silence, and a deer-in-the headlights stare.

Or she'd babble. He'd end up the bewildered recipient of whatever came into her head. *Did you know that shrimp you're tucking into probably came from an uninspected shrimp farm in some godforsaken place in the Far East?* Or, *How do you feel about the destruction of wetlands?*

The result, either way?

Disaster.

It had been the pattern of her life, ever since she'd first noticed that boys were not girls.

The thing was, she wasn't pretty, or clever, or the kind of woman men lusted after. Not that she wanted to be lusted after…

Okay.

A little lust would be nice.

Anna was the pretty one.

She was a great sister and Izzy adored her, but she had long ago faced facts.

Anna was the Orsini sister boys had always noticed.

She was the one with the blond hair, the one who knew, instinctively, what to say and what to wear, who knew how to charm and flirt and turn the most gorgeous guys to putty.

Izzy had long ago accepted the fact that she didn't have those attributes, and she could live with that. What she couldn't live with was turning into a jerk each and every time she found a man attractive.

Speechless or babbling. Those were her choices.

Today's winner was Izzy the Babbler.

She'd already said more to this guy than she should have about his employer. For all she knew, Mr. Heartbreaker might think Rio D'Aquila walked on water.

And now, this—this outburst about him not wearing a shirt…

She swallowed drily and risked a glance at him. He'd stopped laughing. More or less. Actually, she was pretty sure he was choking back another guffaw.

"I'm sorry," she said miserably. "Honestly, I didn't mean—"

"No, you're right." He cleared his throat, rearranged his face until he looked as if he were the one who should do the apologizing. "I was working out back, see, and then I heard the security buzzer go off, and—"

"Really, you don't owe me an explanation. I don't know what I was thinking."

"It's the heat. It makes it hard to think straight."

He flashed a smile that sent her pulse into overdrive. Had she ever seen blue eyes so dark, lashes so long? A woman could hate a man for having lashes like those.

"And you proved it."

Isabella blinked. "Proved what?"

"That it's too hot to think straight. So here's what I suggest. Instead of standing in the foyer, why don't we head for the kitchen? On the way, I'll take a quick detour, grab a clean shirt, and then I'll get us a couple of cold drinks, and—"

"Really, that's not necessary," she said quickly. "You go on. I mean, get yourself something cold.

And a shirt." She blushed. "I mean—I mean, I'll just wait here while you tell Mr. D'Aquila that I'm…" Her eyebrows rose, even as her heart sank. "What?"

"I'm afraid I can't do that."

"Can't do what?"

"I can't pass on your message." He paused. "Mr. D'Aquila isn't here."

"He isn't?"

"No," Rio said, and Isabella Orsini's face fell.

Well, so what?

He'd been cooling his heels for hours, waiting for her to turn up. Now she was upset that the man she'd come to see wasn't available.

Tough.

He wasn't in the mood to conduct an interview now. Besides, only a fool would contract with a workman—a workwoman—*Cristo,* maybe the sun really was getting to him. The point was, even if she had the necessary credentials—and it was an excellent bet that she didn't—he would never deal with a contractor who could not adhere to a schedule.

"He left about an hour ago," he said, and watched

as she sank what looked like perfect white teeth into the soft fullness of her bottom lip.

Rio's gut tightened.

And that was a second excellent reason for not even considering hiring her.

The last thing he needed was to be attracted to a woman who worked for him, although what there was for him to be attracted to was beyond him to comprehend. There were things to like about her he had to admit. She spoke her mind. Those comments about his boss...

Well, no.

Not about his boss. About him. About the powerful, king-of-the-mountain Rio D'Aquila.

And then there was the shirt thing.

He couldn't think of a woman he'd ever known who'd have been embarrassed by his standing around without a shirt. And she had, indeed, been embarrassed. Stripes of crimson had risen along her sculpted cheeks.

Not that her cheeks, sculpted or otherwise, mattered.

She had a forlorn expression on her face now. Her mouth had taken a downward curve.

That made-for-sin mouth.

That silken-looking mouth.

What would she do if he bent his head and put his lips on hers? If he tasted that rosy-pink soft-ness? If he tasted her.

Rio's anatomy responded with alarming speed. He swung away from her, feigned bending to pluck a bit of nonexistent dirt from the gleaming marble floor.

The sun had, indeed, fried his brain.

Why else react to her? She was not his type at all. He'd already admitted that once you got past the shapeless suit and pulled back hair she was pretty, he had to give her that, but a pretty face was not enough.

He liked his women sophisticated. Urbane. Sure of themselves. He liked them in silk and satin. He liked them capable of keeping up a conversation, okay, not about anything weighty but a conversa-tion, nevertheless.

Isabella Orsini flunked all those categories. Plus, she'd wasted his afternoon and was well on the way to wasting his evening—but he wasn't going to let that happen.

He wanted a shower and a cold beer, not neces-sarily in that order. Then he'd head for Easthampton, fly back to the city and never mind staying overnight here or wanting a break in the endless routine of dinner—theater—clubbing. He'd phone a woman, maybe the blonde he'd met last week at that charity thing, ask her if she was busy tonight even though he knew damned well she wouldn't be, women never were when it came to interrupting their lives to accommodate him.

As for the lie he'd told Isabella Orsini about himself—it had been childish nonsense. Why had he done it? To get even with her? Whatever, it had been stupid.

Enough, Rio thought, and he turned and looked straight at her.

The woebegone look had been replaced by one of cool determination. Now what? he thought, and decided to not wait for the answer but, instead, to go straight to the truth.

"Ms. Orsini—"

"Izzy."

"Ms. Orsini," he said, with cool deliberation, "I haven't been entirely straightforward with you." An understatement, but what the hell? "What I said about Rio D'Aquila—"

"I know. You already said he isn't here."

"Right. But—"

"When will he be back?"

Aha. That explained the determined expression on her face. She was going to settle in and wait. Well, that wasn't about to happen.

"I'm going to level with you, Ms. Orsini."

"Izzy."

"Izzy. The truth is—"

"He's not coming back."

"No. Well, that isn't exactly what I—"

"He gave up waiting. And I can't blame him."

Her voice had fallen to a husky whisper. Damnit, was she going to cry? He couldn't stand it when women cried. It was always a maneuver to try and get their own way and he was impervious to that time-worn trick.

"I can't blame him at all."

Dio, better tears than this low, sad tone.

"Look, Ms. Orsini. I mean, Isabella—"

"It's Izzy. Nobody ever calls me 'Isabella.'"

Impossible. She wasn't an "Izzy." "Isabella" suited her better. Maybe she wasn't beautiful but she had a sweet voice, a pretty-enough face…

Rio acted on instinct. He reached out, cupped her chin, raised her face to his.

"Hey," he said, and suddenly he knew he'd been all wrong, thinking her pretty.

She wasn't. She wasn't even beautiful.

She was something more.

How had he missed it? Had he been put off by the game? By his own anger? By her silly outfit?

For the first time, he saw her as she was. The thick, dark lashes. The high cheekbones. That lush mouth. A nose that wasn't perfect; it had a tiny bump in the middle and, somehow, that made it perfect for her.

And, *Cristo,* her eyes.

Green. No, blue. Or brown. Or gold. The truth was, they were an amalgam of colors, and suddenly he was eight years old again, a half-starved kid pawing through a Dumpster behind a restaurant, coming across a chunk of strangely shaped glass.

He'd almost tossed it away. He'd had no need for useless things then. He still didn't, all these years later.

But a ray of sun had hit the glass and the prism—he'd later learned that that was what it was—had flamed to life. The sheer brilliance of the colors had stolen his breath.

The same thing happened now.

Rio looked into Isabella Orsini's eyes and what he saw made his heartbeat stumble.

He wanted to kiss her.

Hell, he was going to kiss her.

He was going to do something incredibly stupid and illogical and he was not a man who did things that were either stupid or illogical and, damnit, yes, he thought, dropping his hand to his side and taking a step back, he'd had too much sun.

"What you need to know," he said briskly, "is that Rio D'Aquila and I are—"

"Trust me. I understand. He got tired of waiting and left you to deliver the message. I lost the job. Well, I never had the job but I lost my chance at it, right?"

"Right," Rio said, "except—"

"I can't blame him. I'm, what, two hours late?"

"Three, but—"

"What happened was that I got a late start. A client phoned. We had lots of rain overnight and I'd just planted pansies on his terrace."

"Pansies," Rio said.

"And the rain soaked them, so I had to head into Manhattan to take a quick look. See, my place is in Brooklyn and the traffic… Anyway, I started a little bit late, and then the traffic on the L.I.E. was a nightmare, even worse than in the city, so—"

"The Long Island Expressway is always crowded," Rio said, and wondered why in hell he was letting this conversation continue. Maybe it was her eyes, the way they were fixed on his.

"I should have known. Anna warned me."

"Anna?"

"So did Joey."

"Joey," he repeated, in the tones of a man trying desperately to hang on to his sanity.

"The boy who does my deliveries." Isabella took a breath. "Then I got to Southampton—and I got lost."

"Surely my—my boss's people sent you directions."

"Well, yes. But I forgot to take them with me. The emergency call about those pansies—and then, of course, I was edgy about this interview."

"Edgy about this interview," Rio echoed. *Dio,* he really was turning into a parrot!

"I kept telling myself that I wasn't excited about it. That's even what I told Dante."

At last, a name he recognized.

"And it's what I told Anna."

So much for names he recognized.

"And then there was this rabbit in the road—"

Rabbits in the road, Rio thought. Had he stumbled into Wonderland?

"But the truth is, I really, really, really would have loved this commission." Isabella—he could not possibly think of her as "Izzy"—flung her arms wide, the gesture taking in everything that had drawn him to this place: the sea, the fields, the dunes, the privacy, the clarity of the sky that was rapidly giving up the day with the onset of dusk. "I thought it was worth going after for the money. Well, and the status of doing a job for a hotshot like Rio D'Aquila. I mean, I'm not much for status, but…"

"No," Rio said with a little smile, "I bet you're not."

"But now that I've seen the house, the setting…" A smile lit her face. "It would have been a wonderful challenge! So beautiful! So big! I'll bet the terrace is enormous, too, and I wouldn't have to think about size constraints, or whether or not rain would drain properly. It would be like—like a painter getting the chance to go from miniatures to—to murals!"

Her face glowed. So did her smile. Neither would win her the job or even an interview. Still—

"Would you like to see the terrace?" he heard himself say.

Her teeth sank into her bottom lip again.

"I shouldn't—"

Rio had started the day wearing a blue chambray shirt over the T he'd discarded. Now, he grabbed it from the table where he'd left it, slipped it on and started walking. A couple of seconds went by. Then he heard the sound of her heels tap-tapping after him.

"Maybe just a peek," she said. "I have the dimensions, of course, your employer's people sent them to me, but to see it, really see it—"

They reached the open terrace doors. Rio motioned her through. She moved past him—and tripped in those ridiculously sexy shoes. His hand shot out automatically; he caught her wrist.

Time stood still.

It was a terrible cliché, but it was precisely what happened.

He heard the catch of her breath. Saw her eyes

widen as she looked up at him. The air seemed to shimmer between them.

"It's—it's the shoes," she said unsteadily, "Anna's shoes…"

Anna's shoes, he thought, but mostly he thought, *to hell with it.* He was going to kiss her, just once, and damn the consequences…

Damnit, he thought, and he let go of her, moved past her and stepped outside.

"Here we are," he said briskly.

"Oh," Isabella Orsini whispered, "oh, my."

He swung around. She stood just behind him, hands clasped at her breast.

"Look at the colors," she whispered reverently. "All those endless shades of gold and green and blue."

Rio nodded. "Yeah," he said. "It's—it's nice."

"Nice?" She gave a soft laugh. "It's perfect. I can see Russian olive all around here, and some rhododendron. And azalea, here and here and here."

Her face was as bright as the sun, her smile wide and honest.

"Mistral azalea," she said, and he nodded again as if he knew what she was talking about.

"And some weigela. For the deeper color of the blossoms."

Slowly, speaking the names of plants and trees and flowers as easily as he'd have dropped the names of cargo ships and stocks, Isabella filled his terrace with plants and trees and flowers made so real by her voice, her words, her smile that he could almost see them.

He couldn't take his eyes from her.

All that eagerness, that joy, that animation…

She reached the area where he'd been digging, didn't hesitate, kicked off those dirt-spattered stilettos and stepped, barefoot, into the rich, dark earth.

Or maybe it was nylon-foot, he thought numbly. Not that it mattered. Whatever you called seeing a beautiful woman in an ugly outfit dig her toes into the soil, it finished him.

Rio was lost.

He took a step toward her. She was still talking, the names of plants and shrubs and God-only-knew what tumbling from that sweet-looking mouth.

"Isabella," he said.

Everything he was thinking was in the way he

said her name. He knew she sensed it, too, because she fell silent and swung toward him.

Was she as lost as he?

"Mr. Rossi," she whispered, and the parting of her lips, the breath she took as he reached for her, was all the answer he needed.

"Don't call me that," he said gruffly.

"No," she said, her voice as husky as his, "you're right." They stood an inch apart, her face lifted to his. A little smile curved her lips. "Hello, Matteo."

"Isabella. You don't underst—"

She put a finger against his mouth.

"I don't want to understand," she said, and Rio gave up the battle, gathered Isabella Orsini into his arms, bent his head and kissed her.

CHAPTER FOUR

OHMYGOD, Isabella thought, *ohmygod...*

Matteo's body was hard. His mouth was firm. His arms were like steel bands, holding her to him.

The part of her brain that relied on cool logic said, *Isabella! What on earth are you doing?*

The part that was all female told that other part to shut up.——

She had never been kissed like this. Never. She'd never wanted to be kissed like this...

He nipped lightly at her bottom lip. She knew he wanted her to open her mouth. To let him touch his tongue to hers. She'd never done that in her life. Well, once or twice, but never again. She hadn't liked it, the intrusion, the intimacy—

"Isabella," he whispered, "I want to taste you."

The words made her tremble, though not with fear. She felt the tip of his tongue at the seam of her lips and she parted them and let him in.

Her knees almost buckled.

His taste. Oh, his taste. Clean. Indescribable. And so amazingly sexy. How could she have ever thought having a man's tongue in your mouth was anything but glorious? Now he was framing her face with his hands, tunneling his fingers into her hair. The barrette securing it snapped open, and her wild torrent of dark curls tumbled free.

She moaned with pleasure.

How could the feel of his hands in her hair be so exciting?

"Isabella," he said thickly, and he swept one hand down her spine and pulled her tight against him.

The world began to spin.

His hand on her backside. Cupping over her bottom through the awful wool skirt.

Her body, responding to the urgency of his, her hips lifting, moving against him.

And yet, there was more.

"Kiss me back," he said in a voice rough as sandpaper.

Wasn't she doing that? What did he want her to—

"Let your lips cling to mine."

Hesitantly, perhaps a little inexpertly, she did as he'd asked and his groan told her she'd got it right.

The hard press of his sex against her belly was even greater confirmation.

He groaned again.

Both his hands cupped her bottom and he lifted her off her feet, lifted her into him. Breast against breast. Belly against belly. Hips against hips and, God, that male hardness was growing, growing, pressing into her—

A little knot of fear lodged in Isabella's throat. Things were going fast, so fast, too fast.

She tore her mouth from his.

"Matteo," she gasped. "Matteo, wait—"

But Rio was beyond waiting.

Later, he'd realize he'd been beyond thinking. Something about Isabella Orsini had turned sexual desire into sexual compulsion.

He wrapped one arm under her ass, wrapped the other around the nape of her neck, brought her mouth to his again and went on kissing her, blind to everything but the need burning white-hot within him as he strode back into the house.

"No."

At first, he didn't even hear her. But she said the word again, her voice harsh, her fists beating against his shoulders.

Sanity returned. Rio opened his eyes. Looked at the woman in his arms.

His gut clenched.

Her face was white, her eyes dark pools of terror. He'd seen all kinds of expressions on women's faces but never fear of him. *Dio,* what in hell was he doing?

"Put me down," she said in a paper-thin voice.

He drew a deep, deep breath. "Listen," he said, "Isabella—"

"Put me down!"

He nodded. Set her carefully on her feet. She took a quick step back.

"Are you crazy?" she said shakily.

Rio ran a hand through his hair. "I'm sorry."

"Sorry? You're sorry? That's it? You—you attack me and then you say you're sorry?"

A muscle knotted in his jaw.

"I did not attack you."

"No? Then, how would *you* describe what just— what just happened?"

The muscle in his jaw flickered again. He'd have

described it as a complete loss of control on his part, but that was impossible.

He never lost control.

"I would describe it as a mistake," he said stiffly. "And I apologize."

Isabella blew a curl from her eyes. Calmer now, she folded her arms, glared at him and told herself she was right, that it had been all his fault.

Of course it had.

The way she'd all but thrown herself into his arms, how she'd responded to his kisses, the wildness that had torn free within her—none of that had any relation to what he'd done...

"It's late," she said abruptly. "I have to leave."

"Yes," he said flatly. "You do."

He swung away from her, walked quickly onto the now-dark terrace, scooped up the portfolio she'd dropped, the shoes she'd kicked off and brought them inside. He could hardly wait to get rid of her; he didn't like what had happened, how he'd behaved, and he fought the urge to tell her that this had been as much her fault as his. She'd come at him with such heat, such hunger, never mind her lack of expertise...

Cristo! Her lack of expertise.

Was she a virgin? That was as impossible as his having lost control. There were no virgins over the age of puberty in today's world.

Not that it mattered.

Hell, it damned well *did* matter! He'd never bedded a virgin in his life; he had no intentions of ever bedding one. Women could be foolish enough about sex, turning it into undying expressions of love even when a man made it absolutely clear, from the start, that sex had nothing to do with anything but desire.

But sex with a virgin? The possibilities were enough to make him shudder as he held out the portfolio and shoes.

"Thank you," Isabella said coldly.

"You're welcome," he said, just as coldly.

She snatched her things from his hands, tucked the portfolio under her arm, spent a millisecond debating whether to try and stuff her size eight feet into Anna's size seven shoes and decided there wasn't a way in hell she'd perform that awful little comedy routine while Mr. Centerfold watched.

It was definitely time to go…

Oh, God! Go where? The car. The car!

"I thought you were in a hurry to leave."

She looked up. Mr. Macho was watching her as intently as a cat might watch a mouse.

"I most certainly am," she said, and she turned on her heel—her bare-but-for-her-shredded-panty hose heel… And turned back.

"Be sure and tell Mr. D'Aquila I'm very sorry he wasn't here to meet with me."

The caretaker's lips turned up in a chilly smile.

"Don't you mean, tell him you're sorry you showed up three hours late?"

"I mean exactly what I said, Mr. Rossi. Nothing more, nothing less. Is that clear?"

Silence. Then his dismissive expression wavered and, damnit, he laughed. Laughed!

"Yes, ma'am," he said, standing straight and tossing off a crisp salute.

Isabella wanted to strangle him. Instead, she chose a dignified exit, though dignity was a tough thing to maintain when you were barefoot, when a man's smug laughter followed you…

When you could still feel the heat of his kisses burning on your lips.

Rio watched her go.

An interesting woman, he had to admit. Even

now, as she marched out of his life, back straight, shoulders squared, head up. Even her posture made it clear she'd been wrongfully treated.

That she wasn't wearing shoes spoiled the effect.

It made him grin.

He lost sight of her once she'd turned the corner; a few seconds later, he heard the front door slam hard enough to make it rattle.

Okay.

She was gone.

Good. Excellent. Out of his home, out of his hair, out of his life.

"Good night, Ms. Orsini," he murmured. "It's a pleasure to have seen the last of you."

What time was it, anyway? He'd left his watch somewhere before he'd started digging. Never mind. He'd search for it in the morning. Right now, he was going to have that long-awaited cold beer, take a shower, put together a meal because, by now, he was hungry as a bear. Then he'd drive to the airport.

Forget that.

He was tired. Simpler to spend the night here and fly home in the morning.

Rio yawned, stretched, headed for the kitchen.

There were half a dozen bottles of beer in the fridge; he chose one at random, rummaged in a drawer, found an opener and yanked off the cap.

The first swallow went down cold, wet and welcome. He took another while he tried to find a way to describe the afternoon.

Unusual? Interesting? He smiled. A little of each, all thanks to Isabella Orsini.

He'd expected Izzy the Gardener.

What he'd got was Isabella the—the what?

She was a bundle of contradictions, charming one minute, prickly the next. Businesslike, then bumbling.

Hot as a woman could be, and then as innocent as a virgin. Unless the innocent thing had been an act. Unless she liked playing with fire, or she liked teasing a man until he went berserk, or—

What did it matter? She was gone.

And it was harmless to think about the possibility that she really was innocent.

That he'd have been the first man to touch her. To learn her secrets. To bring her pleasure again and again, because he would have done that, he'd have shown her what passion could be…

Merda.

Rio slapped the bottle on the counter and headed for the stairs. A shower would set things right, followed by the thickest steak in the freezer, and—

And, where was her car?

He paused on the second floor landing.

She'd come by car. She'd told him so, that confused tale about Manhattan traffic and highway traffic and the rabbit. Then, where was it? Why had she come down that long driveway on foot? He hadn't thought about it before but now, he wondered.

Maybe she'd parked outside the gates. He couldn't come up with a reason she would and, anyway, it wasn't his problem.

Not his problem at all.

He went up another few steps.

Yes, but where was her car?

He hesitated. Then he cursed under his breath, went down the steps, pulled open the front door and saw—

Nothing.

An empty driveway. The tall trees that lined it. The iron gate in the distance. Everything seemed eerie under the glow of the outside lights that had automatically come on at dusk.

The area past the gate was black. A moon as thin as the blade of a scythe hung in the sky but it didn't do much to illuminate the night.

Okay. He'd check. Obviously, her car had been parked on the narrow road outside the gate. It, and she, would be long gone but—

But, he'd check.

He trotted down the driveway. Reached the gate. Pushed against it, but the thing had chosen this moment to stay firmly closed. Rio cursed again. Fumbled for the number pad so he could key in the security code. The gate swung slowly open but so what? He had no idea what he was looking for, what he expected to see…

Hell.

A slender figure was marching along the road. A slender, distant figure, lit by a sliver of moonlight ghosting through the trees.

He had no doubt it was Isabella Orsini.

"Idiot," he growled, as he stepped into the middle of the road and shouted her name.

No reaction. Either she hadn't heard him, or she wasn't going to acknowledge that she had.

"Isabella!" he yelled again. "Damnit, Isabella, what the hell do you think you're doing?"

Still no answer. And she didn't stop walking. He knew she'd heard him; he'd shouted loud enough to silence the cricket symphony in the shrubs, but Isabella was not a cricket.

She was a woman determined to prove she was fearless.

Or daft.

Rio's vote was for "daft." A woman alone, on a dark country road…

Grimly, he started after her. He walked fast. Then he trotted. He'd just broken into a run when headlights appeared, coming toward him. Toward her. Their light spilled over her and, for the first time, she hesitated.

The vehicle slowed. She looked at it. The driver must have said something. Did she want a ride, maybe.

Don't say yes, Rio thought, and ran faster. Whatever you do, Iz, do not say—

She wasn't.

She was saying "no." He couldn't hear her but he could see it. She was shaking her head, shaking it harder and now the vehicle stopped—

Rio flew down the road.

* * *

Don't panic.

The words sang in Isabella's head. *Do not panic! Do not let every Grade D horror flick you saw as a teenager take over your common sense.*

The driver who'd pulled over and asked if she needed a ride was just trying to be helpful. That he'd called her "little girl," that he looked like a sumo wrestler version of Jack the Ripper, meant nothing.

Stop that, Isabella!

The man's weight was his affair. And she didn't even know what Jack the Ripper looked like. Nobody did. She was letting her imagination run away with her...

Isabella's heart leaped into her throat.

Sumo Jack opened his door. "You ain't bein' very friendly," he said as he heaved his bulk out of the car, "an' here I am, just tryin' to be helpful."

Isabella's heart leaped in her throat. *Run,* she told herself, *run, run, run...*

"There you are, sweetheart."

That voice. Husky, lightly accented. "Matteo," Isabella sobbed, and went straight into Rio's arms.

Rio held her close against him. His heart was hammering, and not only from his crazed sprint.

"Baby," he murmured, "it's okay."

For a few seconds, nothing existed but the night and the woman burrowing against him. Then, Rio cleared his throat and looked at the guy standing next to a battered pickup. He was big and beefy. Still, under that beef there probably were slabs of muscle, but that wasn't what troubled him.

It was the way the guy stood there, motionless, his eyes hard and fixed on Isabella.

Rio's blood pounded.

I can take you, you SOB, he thought—but what if he couldn't? He wasn't a fool; he knew how to box. He was strong, his body was hard. He knew that fury at what might have happened would fuel him.

But the guy might get lucky, and win the confrontation. And if he did, what would happen to Isabella?

So Rio swallowed his rage, cleared his throat, forced a smile to his lips.

"Thanks, man," he said. Isabella stiffened against him. Rio held her even closer, hoping the unspoken warning to keep quiet would get through to her. "Offering to help my lady was really decent."

Nothing. The hulking figure didn't speak, didn't move.

Isabella shivered.

"We had an argument. She was angry as a hornet and she took off." A quick grin, this one man-to-man. "You know how it goes."

The guy shifted from one massive leg to the other. Rio waited; he was sure the man's brain was as undersized as his body was massive. Would he take the easy out—or would he come at them?

Rio almost wished he would...

No. He couldn't risk something happening to the woman trembling in his arms. Better to give the hulk the chance to hang on to whatever it was he called his honor.

Rio looked into Isabella's face.

"Sweetheart?" She looked up at him. Her eyes were wide with fear. He wanted to kiss her and tell her everything was going to be fine, soothe her until the terror left her and she sighed and melted against him...

But the thing to do now was to get moving.

"Baby," he said, "let's go home, okay?"

The big man in the road shifted his weight again.

"You need to keep an eye on your woman," he said in a low voice. "Anythin' can happen, a woman walkin' around alone out here at night."

Rio nodded. "Yeah. Thanks again. You take care, dude, okay?" He slid his arm to Isabella's waist. "Come on," he said so quietly that only she would hear him. "Start walking. Come on, Iz. That's it. Left. Right. Left. Right. Faster. The way you did when you and your ego marched out of my house."

That did it.

He felt the strength coming back into her. She'd have jerked away, but he'd expected her to react, hell, he'd counted on it, and he kept her where he wanted her, right in the curve of his arm.

"My ego had nothing to do with it," she whispered, but without as much heat as he'd have liked.

"We can argue that later. For now, just keep going."

"Is he—is he going to let us?"

"He will, if he's got half a brain. He knows I'll plaster the road with him if he tries anything."

"He outweighs you by two hundred pounds."

"Three," Rio said, "but who's counting?"

She gave a watery little laugh, which was what

he'd hoped. The last thing he needed was for her to go into shock.

They walked. And walked, both of them listening for the truck, waiting for it to pass them. The gate was only a couple of hundred yards away but it seemed like miles.

Isabella's footsteps became hurried. Rio held her steady.

"Slow down. That's it. Just stay at an even pace. We're just a couple who made up after a quarrel and we're on our happy way home."

"If only he'd pass us—"

The pickup did, roaring by just as they reached the gate, its oversize tires kicking up a swirl of dust and leaves. Rio shoved her through, locked the gate after them, and Isabella flung her arms around him.

He stood absolutely still for what seemed a very long time. Then he gathered her against him, tilted her face to his and gently brushed his lips over hers.

"Easy, *cara*," he said softly. "Everything's fine now."

"Ohmygod," she said, her voice shaking, "ohmygod…"

Her face was pale, her eyes enormous. He wanted to kiss her again, kiss her until the fear left her, until she clung to him not just for comfort but for the pleasure of being wrapped in his arms.

The thought made no sense and he knew it. He dealt with it by frowning, clasping her elbows and giving her a not-too-gentle shake.

"What in hell were you thinking? This isn't a city, or hadn't you noticed? There are no side-walks, no people, no lights!"

"Oh, that's it! Blame me when it's your fault that—that—" The false bravado faded. "I didn't think," she whispered. "I just wanted to—to get away. To find the train station."

Rio blinked. "The train station? I thought you came by car."

"I did. It wasn't mine. It was—"

"Anna's," he said carefully.

"Yes. But—it drove into a ditch."

Despite everything, Rio had to laugh.

"The car drove itself into a ditch?"

"I told you, there was a rabbit in the road. I think it was a rabbit. It had a long, skinny nose and a long, skinny tail, and it just suddenly appeared in front of me."

"An opossum," he said, as if it mattered.

"And, of course, I didn't want to hit it."

Rio thought of the possum carcasses that littered every country road he'd ever seen, of the trucks and cars that hit them, of the drivers who never noticed or, if they noticed, never cared.

Without thinking, he drew her close again, stroked his hand down her back.

"No," he said carefully, "of course you didn't."

"So the car sort of, it sort of lost direction, and—"

"Where was this?"

"A long way from here. I had to walk. It's why I was so late."

"Why didn't you phone? You do have a mobile phone, don't you?"

"I didn't want to ask Mr. D'Aquila for help. I didn't want to give him any reason to doubt my ability to handle things."

"Right. Which is why you figured being three hours late was better than calling and saying you needed a lift."

Her eyes narrowed. She flattened her hands against his chest and managed to put some distance between them, but only because he let her.

"Thank you for your help, Mr. Rossi."

"What happened to Matteo?"

"You can let go of me now."

"So you can do what? Go for another moonlight stroll?"

Her teeth worried her bottom lip. She had a habit of doing that. He had a habit of wanting to kiss her whenever she did.

"I'll take a bus."

He laughed, and her eyes narrowed.

"No buses? Fine. I'll phone for a taxi."

He laughed again. Her eyes got even narrower. By now, they were icy slits.

"Ask nicely," he said, "and I'll drive you to the railroad station."

The look she gave him suggested that she really wanted to ask him to do something anatomically impossible. He kept his face expressionless as he watched her struggle for control. Finally, she nodded in cool assent.

"I need a ride to the station."

"That's it? That's asking nicely?"

Any minute now, she was going to slug him. The thought made his lips twitch.

"Mr. Rossi. Would you be so kind as to drive me to the station?"

He knew what response he wanted to make. *No,* he'd say, *why should I do that when you can spend the night right here, in my bed?*

Hell, he thought, and let go of her.

"No problem," he said briskly, and headed toward the house and his truck, still parked in the driveway. She followed him and he opened the passenger door, left her to get inside on her own because touching her right now didn't seem a good idea, went around to the driver's side and slid behind the wheel.

They made the drive to town in silence. The place was buttoned up for the night. He put the windows down and heard crickets and the wind and, under it all, the distant sound of the sea.

When they reached the station, he shut off the engine and turned toward her.

"You want to tell me the location of that car-eating ditch?"

The look she shot him would have put glaciers on his stretch of beach.

"No."

Rio shrugged. "Your choice. I figured I'd arrange for a tow but if you'd rather do it—"

"Good night, Mr. Rossi. I'd say thanks for everything but except for you coming along when I was having that—that conversation with that gentleman—"

"Nothing like a nice chat with a homicidal Neanderthal on a dark, deserted road," Rio said lightly, as he went around to her side of the truck.

"I do not require your assistance."

"No, I'm sure you don't. Still, it's late, the area is deserted, and though you may be up for another talk with a *gentleman* determined to prove himself harmless, I'm not. So give us both a break and behave while I walk you inside, okay?"

Isabella glared at the man holding her arm as if he owned her.

Matteo Rossi was insufferable!

If Rio D'Aquila was an arrogant bastard, she could only imagine what he must be like if he could tolerate having someone like this work for him.

Still, there was something reassuring about Matteo Rossi's hand at her elbow. It was late, it was dark, the place had a forlorn air to it but it

wouldn't, not once she was on the station plat-
form. Surely, there'd be other passengers waiting...

Wrong.

There was a sign on the ticket booth.

Closed.

There would be no westbound trains to Penn
Station tonight.

CHAPTER FIVE

ISABELLA stared at the sign.

Impossible. A train station, closed?

She went to the door, tried to force it open. It didn't budge.

It was true, she thought numbly. Your heart really could drop to your toes.

Matteo, standing just behind her, muttered a word she couldn't decipher. Just as well. It probably would have turned the tips of her ears pink.

And no wonder.

He was as eager to see her gone as she was to go.

"It can't be closed," she said, looking over her shoulder at him. "Trains run twenty-four hours a day."

Rio's thoughts were racing. Now what? He walked to the door and tried it.

It was locked.

"Subway trains run twenty-four hours a day,"

he said. "But this isn't a subway, and it isn't Manhattan."

She looked at him and all but rolled her eyes. He couldn't blame her. Talk about useless comments...

And why had he done something so foolish as trying the door himself? Not foolish on the face of it, okay, but he'd had to close the slight distance between them and now he could feel her against him, smell her hair. Lemons? Something light and clean and feminine and, *Dio,* his all-male-all-the-time brain had gone to far more primitive stuff than what to do about this newest problem.

He took a step back, drew in a head-clearing breath of cool night air.

"This is turning into a comedy of errors," she said coldly. "First the car. Then your employer not even having the courtesy to wait for me. Then you. And now, this."

Rio bit back a groan. This was impossible. Who did he stand up for, himself—or himself? She'd just insulted both of them. But that was good. It brought him back to reality.

"Your car went off the road. Oh, sorry. It drove itself off the road. Never mind the rest—the traffic you should have anticipated, the directions you forgot to take with you. The point is, if you still had a car, we wouldn't be standing in the middle of town, waiting for a train that isn't going to come."

She gave him a cold glare. Then she sighed and the glare turned into a sorrowful admission that what he'd said was true.

"You're right. The only person to blame is me for agreeing to try for this job in the first place. I told Gaby it was crazy."

Gaby. A new name added to the mix. Was she referring to Gabriella Orsini, Dante's wife? Rio D'Aquila, who knew the couple, could have asked.

Matteo Rossi, who'd never heard of them, couldn't.

"And Anna. I told her the same thing. 'This job isn't for me,' I said, but did either of them listen?"

Anna, again. The mysterious Anna, so generous with her clothes and her car.

"No," Isabella said grimly, answering her own question, "they did not. They badgered me and badgered me." Her voice went from its soft, pleasing midrange to a high-pitched parody of what he figured was supposed to be Anna-Gaby. "'Think of the doors a contract like that will open, Izzy. Think of the new clients you'll get.'" Her eyebrows drew together. "Ha!"

"Well," Rio said cautiously, "they were probably right."

She snorted with derision. "Bad enough I have to deal with spoiled rich guys in the city. Why should I have to come all the way to the ends of the earth to deal with one in a place where— where creatures rule the road and trains stop running just because it's dark?"

Rio considered pointing out that creatures ruled the road everywhere, and that the dark had nothing to do with trains not running here on a Friday night.

Instead, he took the low ground.

"You have no way of knowing that Rio D'Aquila is spoiled."

"He's loaded," Isabella snapped. "And a hunk."

Rio's eyebrows rose. "Is he," he said.

"Gaby says he is. Anna's never met him but she saw him at a couple of places. Some charity party, the symphony, who knows what? The point is, she saw him. And she said yes, he's gorgeous.

And that he obviously has more money than he needs, and an ego bigger than his head."

Rio folded his arms and made a mental note to add Anna to the list of people he could live without meeting.

"Interesting," he said coldly.

"Maybe she didn't say that, exactly. But why else would he build a house in the middle of nowhere when he already has God only knows how many other houses?"

"Southampton is hardly the middle of nowhere. And, ah, perhaps he found something about the area appealing."

"Do not," she said, chin lifted, eyes blazing, "do not defend your boss to me! I know what men like him are like. I work for them. Well, not on a job anywhere near the size this one is, I mean, the size this one would have been, I mean, the size it would have been if I'd gotten it—"

"I get the picture," he said drily. "So, men who have money are acquisitive fools?"

"Their egos are bigger than their heads."

"An interesting observation."

"A valid one."

"And that includes Dante Orsini, who recommended you for this position?"

Her eyes narrowed. "How do you know that?"

Idiot! "D'Aquila mentioned it."

"No, it doesn't include Dante. Of course it doesn't—but that's beside the point." Isabella shivered. The night air was surprisingly cool. "I am trapped, do you hear me? Trapped in this— this last outpost of civilization!"

It was hard not to laugh. Harder still not to kiss away the angry set of her lips, the flush in her cheeks, the glitter in her eyes.

Damnit, Rio thought, and reached for her and drew her into his arms.

"What are you doing?"

"You're shivering," he said reasonably. "I'm warming you."

"I do not need warming."

"Yes. You do. Stop fighting me and let me chase away the chill."

She stood within his embrace as rigidly as a tree. He held on to her with the determination of a Boy Scout doing a good deed—except, he had never been a Boy Scout and it was hard to think like one now. Isabella felt warm and soft. She smelled sweet and feminine. He wanted to put his lips against her hair. Lift her face to his and kiss her. He wanted to do all the things a man wanted to do to a woman who drove him crazy—

And made him feel something for her that could only be described as tenderness.

He told himself to let go of her and step back— but right at that instant, she gave a weary sigh and put her head against his chest.

Rio shut his eyes and held her closer.

"You're right," she said in a shaky whisper. "I screwed up and I'm stranded. What am I going to do now?"

He had the answer, of course.

He was Rio D'Aquila. He had a plane parked at an airport a short drive away. All they had to do was get into his truck, drive to Easthampton. An hour from now, she'd be where she wanted to be.

In the city.

So, what if he wanted her here?

There was no logic to it. He understood that. What he didn't understand was why logic didn't seem to mean a damn.

Never mind holding her to keep her warm. He

was holding her because she felt so right in his arms—and what was that all about?

For what had to be the thousandth time since Isabella Orsini had walked into his life, Rio told himself that enough was enough. This foolish self-indulgence had to stop. It was time to do the logical thing. To take her to New York. It wasn't only logical, it was the right thing. All he had to do was take the first step.

The problem was, that first step was a killer.

He'd have to tell her who he really was.

The odds were good she wouldn't be happy when he revealed that this had all been a charade. Wouldn't be happy? The understatement of the year. Of the decade.

She'd be furious.

But he could get her past that. Hadn't he charmed CEOs and CFOs and COOs from here to Timbuktu into agreeing to deals they'd started out refusing?

Still, once she knew who he was, everything would change.

She'd still be Izzy the Gardener, with her ruined borrowed car and her ruined borrowed clothes and he—

He would be a liar. A rich liar. A man with too much money and an ego bigger than his head.

If only he had not lied to her. He wasn't even sure what had prompted him to do it. Boredom? Irritation? Just plain perversity? Whatever the reason, this had begun as a silly game.

But it had somehow become more.

Aside from the enormity of living a lie, he felt— he felt wonderful. Relaxed. Content. *Dio,* a few hours ago, he wasn't sure he could even have defined that word.

Most of all, he was enjoying Isabella's company. She was prickly and difficult and argumentative, but she was also gentle and honest and she made him smile.

He felt at ease with her in a way he had not felt with a woman in years.

In his teens and early twenties, when he hadn't had any money, women had been drawn to him because of how he looked. He'd known it and he hadn't much cared. What young guy would? The important thing had been to bed beautiful woman after beautiful woman; his hormones had ruled him.

Then his life changed. Hard work, good luck,

some admittedly clever and dangerous risks, and he'd begun amassing a fortune. He still had the good looks—why be modest over a simple genetic fact?—but now he had money, too, and that ineffable thing called power.

People began treating him differently, especially women.

They were deferential. Eager to please. And always planning how to handle him.

At times, he could almost see them trying to figure out what response he wanted to a simple question. "Would you like to go to the opera tonight, or shall I get tickets for Eric Clapton?" Or, "Are you in the mood for seafood tonight?" Their smiles would freeze. They would hesitate. He knew they were wondering what he wanted them to say, as if there were a correct answer and it would win them a prize.

Perhaps that was the reason he didn't find many of them interesting anymore.

Isabella, on the other hand, was more than interesting.

She was fascinating. And she treated him without pretence.

He couldn't imagine another woman scowling

at him, or arguing with him, or turning her back on him and walking off into a dangerous night.

He certainly couldn't imagine another woman tearing herself from his arms as she had done. Not because he was sure he was such a good lover—although he hoped he was—but because of who he was. Rio D'Aquila, who had an overblown ego and too much money.

But that was the point, after all.

He wasn't that man to Isabella. He was a caretaker. And she liked him for himself. Or didn't like him, as the spirit moved her.

And he loved it.

It was a new world for him, a place where a man was a man and a woman was a woman. It was as close to experiencing a real relationship as he'd ever had…

Rio frowned.

If a man actually wanted a relationship.

He most assuredly didn't.

He just liked being with Isabella. Liked holding her. Another minute or two, then he'd pull aside the curtain and reveal himself as the Wizard in the Emerald City. And, no, that hadn't gone so well for the real wizard but the analogy made—

"—sense."

Rio blinked. "Sorry. I was… What did you say?"

"I said, I thought of the only solution that makes sense."

"Oh?"

"I can phone Anna."

"Anna."

"My sister."

Her sister. At least he had part of the puzzle.

"Anna can come and get me. Or her husband."

She was right. That *did* make sense, and he wouldn't have to tell her the truth about himself, but what would it accomplish? Either way, she'd be out of his life tonight…

And he didn't want that.

Not just yet.

"But…" She swallowed audibly. Sank her teeth into her lip and, *Dio,* if she did that one more time, he was not going to be responsible for his actions.

"But?" he prompted.

She sighed. "But then—then everyone will know that I—that I botched this."

Rio felt a quick knot of anger form in his chest. He slid his hands up her arms, to her shoulders.

"Who is 'everyone'? Why would they judge you? Why should you care?"

"My family. And they wouldn't judge me. They'd be upset for me. See, I have four brothers. And a sister. And all of them are so successful but I'm—I'm—"

"You," Rio said fiercely, "are a beautiful, bright, talented woman."

She blushed. "That's very—it's very sweet of you but—"

"It is the truth. I've seen your sketches for the terrace."

"You have?"

Careful, Rio thought, *damnit, man, be careful!*

"Yes. D'Aquila sent them to me. I, ah, I saw the designs of all the applicants. I'll be here, supervising things on his estate, while the landscaping took shape. He thought it would be a good idea if I were familiar with the various plans."

It sounded ridiculous but she bought it. He knew she did, when she smiled.

"Well, then, I'm glad you liked what you saw."

"Very much," he said softly, and fought the urge to draw her into his arms again. "In fact—in fact,

I'm going to recommend my boss set up a second interview."

Her face lit. He gave an inward groan. What in hell kind of spiderweb was he getting into? How could Rio D'Aquila interview her without giving the game away?

Never mind. He'd faced seemingly impossible situations all his life, and managed to handle them. He'd handle this, too—

But not tonight.

"Okay," he said briskly. "So, calling your sister is not a good idea."

Her smile faded. "Not really."

"Well, I have a plan."

"You do?"

"I do." He took her arm and began walking her toward his truck. "I'll put you up for the night."

"Ha!"

Isabella tried to dig her heels into the pavement but they were bare heels, really bare, because by now the feet of her panty hose were completely shredded. Rio got her to the truck without so much as breaking stride, hung on to her with one hand as he opened the passenger door.

"That," she huffed, "is one hell of a plan!"

"Calm down, Ms. Orsini. I have no interest in seducing you."

"I'm supposed to believe that after what happened before?"

He swung her toward him.

"I kissed you. You kissed me. Who, exactly, tried to seduce whom?"

Her face, lit by a streetlamp, turned red.

"I am not spending the night with you."

"Fine." Rio let go of her and folded his arms. "You can spend it here, on a bench. Or would you prefer curling up in the grass?"

She stared at him. He could almost see her brain whirring.

"In the morning," he said, "I'll arrange to have your car taken to a garage. If they can fix it, they will. If they can't, you'll rent another."

"I don't—"

"Don't what?"

She shrugged and looked down at the ground. "Nothing."

Rio rolled his eyes. "You don't have the money for either, and you don't want to ask Anna for help. Am I right?"

Another shrug, even more expressive than the first.

"I'll lend you the money."

She looked up. "You?"

"I'm a caretaker, not a drifter. I have an income. I have some savings."

"I didn't mean—"

"Yes, you did. But those of us who work with our hands are as fiscally and morally responsible as anyone else."

Dio, that sounded impossibly stiff-necked, but it was the truth. Once, he had worked with his hands. Now, he was rich. How had he become so wealthy? How had he accumulated the money to make his first investment? By working hard, living frugally and saving first every lira, then every euro, every Brazilian real that he could.

Isabella hesitated. Then she gave him a smile that lit the night.

"You're a good man, Matteo Rossi. Thank you."

She climbed into the truck. He slammed the door. Then he went around to the driver's side and got behind the wheel.

A good man?

He was a goddamned liar, was what he was.

A good man would have told her the truth. Would have taken her home, or sent her home, because he had enough money to get anyone to do anything at any hour, or so bitter reality had taught him.

Rio started the truck, backed away from the curb.

A good man wouldn't have begun this charade in the first place. At the very least, a good man would have put an end to it by now.

So much for his being a good man.

He'd told her one truth, at least. He would not seduce her. He didn't want to seduce her—

Cristo, at least be honest about that, D'Aquila. A woman who can make your belly knot, your balls ache, with nothing more than a smile? All he wanted was to seduce her.

But he had no intention of even trying.

That scene at the house earlier had been a warning.

She was innocent, or close to it. And he didn't play games with innocent women.

But would a little self-indulgence be wrong? Would it affect anything that mattered to go on letting her think he was the caretaker? Give her a room for the night, a meal, enjoy just talking with her and then send her on her way tomorrow?

No. There was no way it possibly could.

He'd help her with her dilemma, let her think her knight errant was named Matteo, and nobody would be hurt.

Not her.

Not him.

And that would be the end of it.

CHAPTER SIX

THE night was dark, the roads were empty and Isabella's brain was no longer functioning.

How else to explain why she was letting a stranger take her home with him? And what did that mean? Where was his home?

He hadn't said. And she hadn't asked.

No longer functioning, indeed.

She'd assumed he meant they were going to the D'Aquila estate. And wasn't that silly? Assuming anything was generally a mistake. Just look at today, and her assumption that Rio D'Aquila would be waiting to interview her.

Wrong on both counts.

He hadn't been waiting, and she hadn't been interviewed.

Now, she'd assumed spending the night with a man she'd just met was a good idea. But it wasn't. How could it be? He was gorgeous, he was sexy— and for all she knew, he was an ax murderer.

"Relax," he said with lazy humor in his voice. "We're going back to the house. And it's a big house. Four guest suites. You can choose the one you like."

Isabella felt color creep into her face.

"I wasn't—"

"Yes. You were." He glanced at her, his face unreadable in the darkness. "A little late to start wondering if I have ulterior motives, don't you think?"

What she thought was that she didn't need him poking around in her head, or pointing out that she'd just added one more foolish act to a day filled with them.

"You're right," she said sweetly. "I probably should have asked if you turn into a vampire at midnight."

He chuckled. "A hungry vampire. I don't know about you but I can't remember the last time I ate anything today."

Neither could she, but admitting it would just mean he'd scored another small victory in mind reading.

"You must be hungry, too."

"Not at all," she said, with the self-righteousness of a candidate for sainthood.

Unfortunately, her belly chose that moment to growl.

"Obviously not." His tone was wry but, thank God, he didn't laugh. "So, you can just watch me eat. How's that sound?"

Stubbornness was one thing. Stupidity was another. Even she knew that.

"Okay," she said, "you're right. I'm starved. Is there a diner around here? A McD's? My treat."

Her treat.

He wanted to laugh.

Or maybe not.

Women bought him gifts. Nothing new in that. An expensive watch for what one breathlessly called a one month anniversary. A ridiculously expensive case of wine from one lover who'd somehow learned the date of his birthday. From others over the years, a gold pen, sapphire studs, diamond cufflinks.

And each time, he said, "Thank you, it's a wonderful gift, but I can't let you spend your money on me."

The real message was that he would not let a

woman forge a relationship intimate enough for him to accept a gift.

But no woman had ever offered him something like this. A hamburger and fries. He couldn't even imagine any of the women he knew admitting to liking hamburgers and fries.

For the first time in his life, Rio wanted to say yes.

Hell, no.

What he really wanted was to pull to the side of the road and kiss the lovely, messy, quirky, altogether delectable Isabella.

Rio took a deep breath.

And did neither.

Kissing her was absolutely out of the question. Hadn't he made that vow to himself just a few minutes ago?

As for going to a restaurant, even a diner or a fast-food joint…

No way.

He wasn't naive. There were a handful of other places that drew people who shunned publicity. Ski resorts, islands in the sun. He'd been to a few of them, enough to know that a town's laissez-faire attitude toward its rich and famous visitors could change after dark when the movers and shakers of the world vied for just the right table in just the right place.

For all he knew, that even applied to diners and burger places in a town frequented by high-profile names.

The very last thing he wanted was for someone to recognize him now. Living a lie, he thought as his guilty conscience gave a nasty twinge, was not easy.

"Tell you what," he said. "We'll make something when we get home."

"Home? Is that how you think of his estate?"

"Of his… Oh. D'Aquila. Well, sure. I live there."

"Will he object? To you having an overnight guest. I mean—"

"I know what you mean. Just for the record, I haven't had any overnight guests. Not the way you meant it."

"I didn't…"

"You did." His tone roughened. "What you really want to know is have I had a woman stay there with me."

Isabella flushed. "Why would I care?"

"That's an excellent question. Why would you?"

Why indeed? Isabella thought, and searched for an answer that made sense.

"Because—because I'm a little uncomfortable at the thought of staying in a house without the owner knowing it."

It wasn't the answer he'd wanted, and wasn't that ridiculous? This had nothing to do with the reason a man generally takes a woman home with him.

This was about expediency.

There was nothing else he could do with her.

You could tell her the truth.

And his conscience could just shut the hell up. Hadn't he already gone through this internal debate? Hadn't he concluded, and logically so, that there was no harm in continuing the deception for another few hours?

After that, Isabella Orsini would be a memory.

Rio shrugged.

"D'Aquila wouldn't object. Besides, he'll be away for the next few days."

"And you have—what? An apartment over the garage? A house on the grounds?"

The real caretaker lived a couple of miles away, but he could hardly tell her that.

"Over the garage," he said. When it came to telling lies, Pinocchio had nothing on him. "But it isn't finished yet. For the time being, I live in the house itself."

"Your employer doesn't mind?"

"You know," he said carefully, "it might be a mistake to judge men by the size of their bank accounts."

That won him a sigh.

"You sound like Anna."

"Your sister."

"She says I'm too judgmental when it comes to men."

Perhaps this Anna was more insightful than he'd thought.

"A woman like you should be judgmental," he said gruffly.

"A woman like me?"

A woman who's bright and beautiful, innocent and sexy, a woman any man would be taking to his bed and not to a guest room, he almost said. Thankfully, the gate to his estate loomed up just in time.

"A woman on her own," he said, and for once, *grazie a Dio,* the gate opened without difficulty and he put the moment, and the thought, behind him.

Rio headed straight for the kitchen, switched on all the lights, opened the fridge—and then realized Isabella was still standing in the breakfast room that adjoined it.

"Now what?"

She looked at him, then down at herself, then at him again.

"I'm a mess."

She was. A lovely mess, but a mess nonetheless. The torn and stained suit, the smudged blouse, the panty hose with so many runs they looked more like ribbons than nylons.

He was pretty much a mess himself.

"Is there somewhere I can wash up?"

There were five places where she could wash up, five huge bathrooms with five huge tubs and five huge shower stalls, and suddenly he saw himself with her in one of those bathrooms, saw himself slowly undressing her, baring her to his eyes, saw himself lifting her, carrying her into one of those enormous shower stalls, turning on the water so it poured down on them as gently as a summer rain, saw his hands on her breasts, his mouth on her nipples...

"Matteo? If you could just tell me where to find a bathroom..."

"No problem," he said, his voice hoarse, his erection almost painful. It was a damned good thing he was standing behind the open refrigerator door.

He gave it a minute. Then he flashed what he hoped was a smile, shut the door and led her up the stairs to the guest suite farthest from his own rooms, though how in hell he was going to explain his using the master suite was beyond him.

Everything was beyond him now.

He knew it, knew that he should never have brought her here because his vaunted self-control was gone, gone, gone—

"Okay," he said briskly, as he flung open the door to the suite, "there should be clean towels in the bathroom. New toothbrushes, soap, shampoo, all that stuff."

Isabella nodded. "Thank you."

"Hey, don't thank me. Thank the decorator. You

know how these guys are. Somebody tells a guy who has a PhD in ribbons and bows to furnish a house, he goes all the way."

She laughed. Good. Keep it light. Anything to keep his mind from wandering to the one place it wanted to go.

He stepped back.

"The kitchen," he said. "Fifteen minutes."

"Yessir," Isabella said, and gave a quick salute, the same kind he'd given her hours before.

Rio narrowed his eyes. Then he pulled the door shut so hard it sounded like a thunderclap and marched resolutely down the hall.

As soon as the door shut, Isabella sagged back against it and let out a long breath.

The way he'd looked at her right before they'd started talking about toothpaste and towels... The way she'd felt, knowing he was looking at her that way...

Isabella, a stern voice that sounded a lot like Anna's said, *whatever are you doing here?*

The answer was simple.

She was spending the night because her car was in a ditch and the trains weren't running.

Could a voice in your head really say, *Pshaw?* Or as close to *pshaw* as it could get? And, so what if the trains weren't running? A town like this, there were sure to be private car services.

And you didn't think of that until now because...?

Because she couldn't afford the zillion bucks a car service would surely charge for taking her from here to the city, and yes, she had a rich father and rich brothers and a sister who was married to a prince. So what? She'd always insisted on making it on her own.

Damned if she'd stop now.

Isabella turned the lock and began peeling off her clothes. She looked at the suit jacket, then the skirt.

Ugh.

Anna, she decided, using two fingers to pick both items from the tile floor, would surely not want this stuff back. Ditto for the blouse. Grimacing, she dropped all three items into a discreetly disguised wastebasket in the corner of a discreetly disguised bathroom that had been designed to look more like an Asiatic spa than a room meant to contain a tub, a sink, a toilet and a shower.

Not that she'd ever seen an Asiatic spa but if

she ever did, it would probably look like this. At least, she hoped it would. Silk wallpaper meant to look like golden meadow grass. A soaking tub big enough to double as a houseboat. A shower that could easily host a party or, at least, a man and a woman.

A man with dark hair and blue eyes, broad shoulders and narrow hips. Long legs and, wait a minute, what about that square jaw, that tiny scar she'd noticed, that unabashedly sexy grin...

Isabella frowned, peeled off what remained of her panty hose, her bra and her panties—she'd never been sure whether you were supposed to wear them over or under your panty hose but it didn't much matter because she lived in jeans. As for all this stuff, bra and panties and pathetic panty hose—it went into the trash, too.

Soap, she thought. And shampoo. Matteo had said—and yes, once she'd opened a few drawers, she found it all. Soap and shampoo and conditioner, toothpaste and toothbrushes and towels. Big, fluffy towels.

She plucked a wrapped bar of soap from its shelf and sniffed it. Mmm. Vanilla. Were they all...?

No. There were half a dozen different scents. Lemon. Jasmine. Lavender. Tea rose. Ginger.

Lemon, she decided. Lemon was always her favorite. And for her hair… She opened a small bottle and brought it to her nose. Lemon, again.

Perfect.

Did Matteo like the smell of lemon?

Not that it mattered, she thought quickly, as she stepped into the enormous glass shower. Why on earth would it matter? She liked it. That was all that was important. She wasn't interested in Matteo Rossi as a man. Well, he was a man, of course. An incredible man. Gorgeous. Sexy. Funny and clever, but so what?

She wasn't looking for a one-night stand.

Even if she had been—

Matteo wasn't interested in her.

He'd kissed her. So what? You didn't have to be sexually knowledgeable—and, good Lord, there had to be a better way to put it than that—to know that a kiss was just a kiss.

She had four brothers, all of them settled now into happy married lives, but she'd grown up with them, she'd overheard conversations she wasn't supposed to overhear. Meaning, Isabella thought as she rinsed conditioner from her hair, meaning a guy might well kiss a woman for no better reason than because he could.

A good-looking man saw a good-looking woman…

Not that she was good-looking, she thought, catching sight of her reflection in the mirror across from the glass shower stall.

She turned a little. To the side. To the back. To the front again.

Okay. She wasn't beautiful. She wasn't homely. What she was, she decided, was medium.

Medium height. Medium build. Medium everything, legs and hips and breasts.

Would Matteo want to kiss a medium woman? If he saw her now, would he? With her hair loose and wet, the long curls hanging down her back. With her skin glittering with droplets of water. With her nipples tightly budded by the coolness of the water.

Or by imagining him, in the stall with her.

Isabelle moved the soap slowly over her skin.

His body, hard and muscled and sleek, supporting hers as she leaned back against him. His hands, cupping her breasts; his fingers on her nipples. His mouth on the nape of her neck. His leg separating her thighs, and then his hand between them, seeking, finding, touching—

The soap fell from her fingers.

Quickly, she picked it up. Rinsed herself. Shut off the water, grabbed an oversize bath towel and wrapped herself in it as she padded into the bedroom.

Fantasizing about George Clooney was one thing. Not that she ever did but *if* she did, well, George Clooney was George Clooney. A face, a body on the screen.

Matteo Rossi, on the other hand, was a real person. A *real,* real person, someone she knew. Someone in another room, just down the hall, maybe standing in the shower right now, naked…

Isabella bit back a moan.

What was wrong with her?

She didn't think about naked men. She didn't think about men, period. It was silly and she had better things to do with her time, like retrieving the yucky suit and equally yucky blouse from the trash because, damnit, she had nothing else to put on, and the fifteen minutes Matteo had mentioned were just about—

Knock, knock, knock.

Isabella spun toward the door. "Yes?"

"It's me."

Her heart pounded. Matteo. Who else would it be?

"I know." She winced. That was clever. "I mean, I'll be ready in—"

"I have some stuff you can wear."

She blinked. So much for his not having brought women here before.

"Isabella? Open the door."

"No, that's okay. I mean, I don't need—"

"You do," Matteo said, sounding amused. "Unless you really prefer that 'I've been dragged through the mud' look that's so popular this year."

She laughed. Carefully. Not loud enough so he'd hear it, but how could she not laugh at such a perfect description of how she'd certainly looked in what had once been a designer outfit?

She looked down at herself. The towel was tucked tightly under her arms and went all the way down to her knees. She wore less than this to the pool.

"Okay. You want to put that stuff back on, I'll just—"

The door swung open. Wrong. Isabella had cracked it maybe an inch. Rio saw an eye, half a mouth, a tumble of dark, wet curls and a naked shoulder.

A wet naked shoulder.

His mouth went dry.

There was a long silence. Then he cleared his throat and forced his gaze to her face.

"I, ah, I brought you some things."

"What size?"

He blinked. "Excuse me?"

"I wondered what size clothes the women you haven't brought here left be—"

Isabella's voice trailed off. Oh, God! Such a dumb thing to say? What did it matter how many women he invited home? She was spending the night out of expediency, not spending it with him.

"Why, Izzy," he said softly. "You're jealous."

Heat flooded her face. "Certainly not! I simply meant—"

"I know exactly what you meant."

"No," she said quickly, "you don't. Why would I—"

"They're sweats. And socks." He smiled. "Mine."

"Oh. Well, I knew that. I mean, I figured that. I mean—"

Rio put his hand against the door. Before she had time to react, he'd pushed it open, leaned in, bent his head and captured her lips with his.

Dio, she tasted wonderful. Mint toothpaste and essence of Isabella. It was an amazing combination and when she moaned and melted toward him, he dropped the stuff he was holding and wrapped his arms around her.

She was soft. Warm. She smelled of lemon. And he wanted her, wanted her, wanted her…

It took all the willpower he possessed to slowly drop his hands to his sides and step back. Isabella was breathing hard. Well, *merda,* so was he.

"I don't," she whispered, "I really don't understand any of this. I'm not like this. I'm not. I'm really not—"

He bent to her and kissed her again. Deeper. Harder. With a hunger that he knew he'd never felt before. Then he scooped the sweats and socks from the floor and held them toward her. She looked at them. Looked at him. Then, clutching the towel to her with one hand, she took the things and pressed them against her breast.

"I'll meet you in the kitchen," Rio said gruffly.

One last kiss. One soft brush of his lips over hers. Then he stepped away, closed the door...

And wondered what she'd say if he told her he didn't understand any of it, either.

CHAPTER SEVEN

HER knees were wobbly.

Which was silly.

How could a man's kisses turn your knees to jelly?

They did, though. Isabella plopped down on the edge of the bed. Maybe it was safer to contemplate a thing that was clearly a physical impossibility sitting down.

Her lips tingled. Her heart was racing. She was breathing fast. She was a cliché-ridden mess, a bad romantic movie translated from the screen to real life.

Brilliant. Truly brilliant.

The clothes Matteo had given her lay in her lap. She looked down and choked back a laugh. Workout clothing. A sweatshirt and pants, a pair of socks that looked big enough to fit the feet of a yeti.

And she'd accused him of bringing her stuff another woman had worn.

The laugh turned into a groan, and Isabella buried her face in her hands.

Forget silly. She'd gone straight to stupid. Why was he doing this to her? Turning not just her bones but her brain to jelly?

She drew a long, ragged breath, pushed her hair from her eyes and sat up straight.

Except—except he wasn't "doing" anything. Well, he was kissing her, sending shivers up and down her spine each time he did, but she was equally guilty.

She let him do it. Let him? An understatement. She was encouraging him by kissing him back, each and every time.

The why of that was easy.

She was doing it because she loved how he kissed her. How he held her. She loved the feel of his hard body against hers, the heat of his hands, the tightly controlled power she could sense when he held her.

Forget what she'd told herself about his kissing her because he could.

He wanted more. Lots more.

And, oh, my, so did she.

Which was absolutely, totally, completely incomprehensible.

She wasn't the kind who had sexy thoughts. She didn't even have sexy dreams.

You're just inhibited, Iz, Anna had said, a long time back. They'd been in their mid-teens then, other girls talking about boys and sex, Isabella wondering if there was something wrong with her because she'd go to the movies with a boy, go to a school dance, and if her date tried to kiss her she'd imagine what it would feel like, where his lips would go, where hers would go, would she end up, yuck, tasting his spit?

Her solution to the problem was invariably the same. She'd stick out her hand and say *Thanks, tonight was fun,* and the boy would never call again.

You think things to death, Anna had said with the loving wisdom of a sister older by thirteen months and wiser by what sometimes seemed a decade. *Just relax. Learn to let go a little.*

It was good counseling. Isabella had even tried it.

She'd learned to like kissing. Not to love it but

to like it. Closed-mouth kissing, anyway. Eventually, she'd learned to tolerate a fumbled caress.

A couple of times, she'd let guys take things a little further. Open her bra. Touch her breasts. Watched, with a kind of clinical fascination, as their faces grew flushed, their breathing unsteady, while nothing even close was happening to her.

All she'd felt, each time, was embarrassed.

Finally, with all the grim determination of a woman going for a root canal, she'd decided it was time to have sex. Maybe the experience would turn out to be, well, liberating.

She'd gone to bed with a nice guy, the accountant who did her taxes. When it was over, she was out one lover…

And one accountant.

Which was when she'd decided to put sex and passion and all that nonsense out of her mind.

Until now.

Isabella drew another deep breath.

"Enough," she told the silent room.

Everything in life had a logical explanation. So did her behavior. She was hungry. Starved, was closer to accurate. That explained a lot. She might even be dehydrated.

A meal. Lots of water. After that, she'd be fine.

The thing to do was get dressed, put on Matteo's sweat suit and his socks. A classy, sexy outfit, for sure, she thought with a little smile, which was fine because sex and sexiness had nothing to with the reason she was spending the night.

Then, she'd head downstairs, help him put together some kind of supper. Sandwiches, soup, whatever. They'd eat, be casual about it, talk about banal things and then she'd come back up here, go to sleep and that would be the end of whatever was going on.

Because nothing was.

Okay. There was a little chemistry. She could admit that, she thought as she put on the clothes. And it was—it was fun, especially when you'd never had chemistry with a man before. Under the right circumstances, she just might find flirting, even sex, well, interesting.

Don't you mean, sex with the right man, Isabella?

"The right man has nothing to do with it," she said in a firm voice.

Liar, the little voice inside her whispered.

Isabella told it to shut up.

Then she opened the door and went in search of the kitchen.

Rio knew as much about kitchens as a lion would know about a canary.

This kitchen, especially. He'd told the architect to come up with a kitchen that would suit the house.

The result was this enormous room, a long stretch of stainless steel appliances that would have made a master chef smile, a variety of machines that baffled him, and the kind of lighting he figured surgeons would want in an operating room.

Merda!

He flicked switches, dimmers, took the lights down to a bearable level and thought how great it would be if he could do the same thing with his libido.

Damnit, he thought, as he opened the refrigerator, this nonsense had to stop!

He had not brought Isabella here to have sex with her.

Not that he hadn't thought of it endlessly most

of the day but he'd reached a decision. There wouldn't be any sex. It was an excellent decision, and if he could just stop touching her, he would not have a problem over having reached it.

He'd brought her home with him because she had no place else to go.

Well, not exactly.

He could have flown her to New York. Or hired a limo. But then the proverbial cat would have been out of the proverbial bag.

There was no reason to tell her anything.

After tomorrow morning, he would never see her again.

Where were those steaks his caretaker had said he'd bought? Where would you put a steak, in a fridge big enough to house a family of six and all their friends and relatives?

Right there. Inside a clear plastic drawer. And, in another drawer just below, there were lettuce and tomatoes and corn, things he'd almost forgotten the caretaker had mentioned hours ago. A lifetime ago, was more the way it felt.

Isabella had come walking up that driveway and ushered in a new dimension of time.

Which had nothing to do with turning this stuff

into something resembling a late supper. And that was important because he needed a solid meal. Get something in his belly, he'd be able to think straight.

He'd made a decision and he was sticking to it.

No sex, he thought firmly, as he put the steaks on the stone counter beside the stove. It sounded like the title of a bad French farce—except there was nothing amusing about it.

Isabella was innocent. In spirit if not in fact. And he wasn't into deflowering virgins or introducing inexperienced women to the pleasures of sex, no matter how willing the women might seem.

Rio's mouth went dry.

And, *Cristo,* she was willing.

He could not think of a woman who had ever been more responsive to his caresses. He could imagine her in his bed, opening her arms to him as he slid between her thighs, as he filled her with his desire, his heat…

With the major hard-on that had just come to immediate life in his sweatpants.

Food. He needed a meal. So did she. A solid night's sleep afterward and tomorrow, life would return to normal. She'd be back in New York and he—he'd be Rio D'Aquila again, because that was who he was. Not Matteo Rossi. He had not been Matteo Rossi for years and he'd be glad to get rid of him, for all time.

It would be a welcome relief.

The Viking stove had a built-in grill. He turned it on, then filled a pot with water and put it on to boil. He husked two ears of corn, checked the heat of the grill, slapped the steaks on it, found the water bubbling and dumped in the corn.

So much for putting a meal together, and wasn't it a lucky thing his caretaker had bought steaks because steak, scrambled eggs and grilled cheese sandwiches constituted Rio's entire kitchen repertoire.

Matteo Rossi had known how to cook. Not well, but well enough. He'd known how to make pasta sauce, chili, hamburgers, even omelets. When a man had to fend for himself and do it on the cheap...

Dio! Who gave a damn about any of that now? Why even think about it, when you had housekeepers and cooks?

He found the bottles of wine. A pair of reds,

pinot noirs that carried the label of a noted South Shore vineyard. He uncorked one, set it aside to breathe; yanked open cabinets and drawers, found heavy white stoneware, equally heavy flatware, white linen napkins and salt and pepper mills. He opened another cabinet, found a pair of thin-stemmed red wineglasses…

And thought, *What the bloody hell am I doing?*

He stood still, put his hands on his hips and took a couple of deep breaths.

He was bustling around like a demented Julia Child, and for what? This was a late supper borne of necessity. It wasn't a romantic dinner for lovers.

He and Isabella were not lovers. They would not be lovers. All he had to do was get that final image of her out of his head. Her, wrapped in that towel, her hair damp and wild and sexy, water pearling on her shoulders, her eyes blurred and filled with him as he drew her to him and claimed her mouth…

"Hi."

Rio swung around.

Isabella stood just inside the kitchen. Her face was shiny. Her curls were out of control. Her sweats—his sweats—dwarfed her. The socks were the finishing touch. They reminded him of the kind of things clowns wore on their feet: long, loose and oversize.

No designer outfit. No fifteen hundred dollar blowout that would have taken away those beautiful curls. No makeup so artfully applied that he was never supposed to know it had taken an hour to do.

Just this.

Just Isabella.

His heart turned over.

He wanted to go to her, kiss that naked mouth, that shiny face, plunge his hands deep into that tumult of untamed curls…

For God's sake, D'Aquila. Weren't you paying attention to yourself? None of that is going to happen.

When he didn't answer, she colored a little and forced a laugh.

"Not exactly a *Vogue* cover, huh?"

He knew the correct, gentlemanly response. He was supposed to say she looked precisely like a *Vogue* cover but hell, he wasn't a gentleman, he was Matteo Rossi who'd grown up in an orphanage and had worked with his hands.

"No," he said a little hoarsely, "not a *Vogue* cover."

Her smile dimmed and he walked slowly toward her.

"You're far more beautiful that any cover, *cara,*" he said softly, and what could he do then but frame her face in his hands and kiss her?

It was a light kiss, the whisper of his lips against hers, but it made him groan.

He wanted more. He wanted everything and from the way she responded, holding back for a heartbeat, then rising on her toes, sighing against his mouth, parting her lips to his, so did she.

Matteo groaned again and slid a hand under her sweatshirt. She gasped as his fingers skated over the silken flesh of one breast, moaned as they danced across the nipple.

"Matteo," she whispered, "oh, God, Matteo…"

His body clenched like a fist. He lifted his head, looked blindly into her eyes. Then he drew his hand out from under her shirt and walked away.

When he reached one of the stone counters, he clutched the edge with both hands, waited for his heartbeat to return to something approaching normal. When it did, he faced her again.

She was standing as he'd left her, her eyes enormous, her lips slightly parted. Desire, fierce and hot, swept through him but he fought it and jerked his chin toward the plates and other things he'd set aside.

"Supper's almost ready," he said briskly. "How about setting the table?"

He saw her throat constrict as she swallowed. She swayed a little. Then she flashed a smile that he knew was as phony as his casually phrased request.

"Sure," she said, and when she turned away and went to do as he'd asked, it was all he could do not to go after her, swing her into his arms and carry her to his bed.

They ate, or pretended to eat, in a strained silence broken only by Isabella's polite, "This is very good," and his equally polite, "I'm glad you like it." Rio poured the wine but after a couple of obligatory sips, neither of them touched their glasses.

Finally, she put her knife and fork across her plate, touched her lips with her napkin and set it beside the plate.

"You know," she said, "it turns out that I'm not very—"

"No. Neither am I."

She pushed back her chair. He followed. They rose to their feet.

"I'll help you clean up," she said.

"No," he said quickly. "I'll take care of it. You go on to bed. You must be exhausted."

She nodded. "I am. Yes. I—I—"

Ah, sweet Mary, she looked so lost.

"Isabella," he said in a low voice.

She looked up at him. Her eyes were shiny with unshed tears.

"I was a fool to come here," she whispered.

"No. You weren't. I'm the fool. I shouldn't have—"

"You were kind. You took in a stray, and I— I've overstayed my welcome."

"Isabella—"

"It doesn't matter. I'll be out of your way first thing in the morning. I've thought it through and it's ridiculous for me not to phone my sister. She'll come get me and—"

"You don't need her. I'll take care of it."

She shook her head. "I'm not about to let you drive me all the way to the city."

"It's not that far."

"It's a couple of hours. At least. If there's traffic—"

"Hell, what do I care about traffic? I'll take care of you."

"I don't need anyone to take care of me."

"Yes. You do." Rio pushed aside the chair that separated them. "And I'm the one who's going to do it."

Isabella could feel fury growing inside her. He'd been taking care of her, all right, first driving her half out of her mind with his kisses, then turning cool and distant. Did he think she was a child?

Because she damned well wasn't.

"Look," he said, his tone so conciliatory it made her teeth grind together, "we shouldn't be having this conversation. It's late. You're tired. And—"

"And what?" She closed the small distance between them, chin up, eyes molten gold, everything about her ready for a fight. "You think I don't know what's going on? That for all your Good Samaritan talk, you're sorry as hell you ended up in this mess?"

"What mess?" He was bewildered. What the hell was she so angry about? "All I did was—damnit, I don't know what I did! What's got you so ticked off?"

"Me?" Isabella poked a finger into the center of his chest. "I am *not* ticked off. You are. And I know the reason. You've been stuck with me the entire day. And I haven't tumbled into bed with you when you made those pathetic moves on me and—"

"Pathetic moves?"

She blinked. Had she actually said that? Hadn't she just finished telling herself he was the one who'd backed off after each kiss? It was one or the other, she thought grimly, and what did it matter which?

"Pathetic moves," she repeated recklessly, despite the swift glimmer of anger in his eyes. "That's what I said."

Rio's jaw shot forward. "Damnit, woman," he said, grabbing her wrist, "do not poke your finger at me! And do not twist the truth. If my moves were so pathetic—and, trust me, Ms. Orsini, they weren't 'moves' at all—if they were, how come you responded by climbing all over me?"

That made her eyes flash. Good. Why should she be the only one hurling insults?

"You're joking. I climbed all over you?"

"Like tonight, when I brought you that clothing. There I was, being, yes, a Good Samaritan, and how did you respond?" He lowered his head until they were eye to eye. "Like a cat in heat on a back alley fence, that's how."

Her face turned crimson.

"You," she said in a voice that trembled, "are a horrible man."

"Oh, I must be," Rio snarled. "Hell, only a horrible man would tolerate the presence of a woman who showed up for an appointment six hours late."

"Two. And what's it to you? I wasn't supposed to meet with you, I was meeting with your full-of-himself boss."

"Three, and you don't know a thing about my boss."

"I know all I need to know."

"For instance?"

"He's pretentious."

Rio's eyes narrowed. "The hell he is."

"He's a cold-hearted SOB."

"And you know this, how?"

"I just do," Isabella snapped.

"Oh, that's brilliant. 'I just do,'" Rio said, mimicking her in a faux soprano that made Isabella want to scream.

The fact was, everything about him made her want to scream.

How could she have even imagined wanting to go to bed with him? He wasn't only horrible. He was arrogant and disgustingly macho and he twisted every word, every situation, to his own ends.

"You," Isabella said, her nose an inch from his, "are an arrogant example of everything I despise! You—you toady to the rich, you make excuses for them—"

"Don't hold back," Rio said coldly. "Not on my account."

"You dance to your boss's tune because he lets you play at being him. Just look at you, living in his house, eating his food, drinking his wine… What are you laughing at? Damnit," she shrieked, "do not laugh at me, Rossi. Do not dare laugh at—"

Rio pulled her into his arms.

"Let go," she demanded, but he'd had enough.

He kissed her. And she went up in flames.

She grasped his shirt. Rose on her toes. Opened her mouth to his and sank her teeth delicately, deliciously into his bottom lip. She moaned. Whimpered. Pressed her body to his and he knew he was done pretending he didn't want her.

Rio thrust his hands deep into her hair and lifted her against him. She cried out and ground her hips against his erection.

This, he thought, this was the one real thing, the one honest thing between them.

"Matteo," she moaned, and even that was all right. He *was* Matteo Rossi; he was more him tonight than he had ever been Rio D'Aquila.

He drew back, just enough to look into her eyes, and any last remaining anger flew away.

"Isabella. *Cara mia. Bella mia.*" He ran his hand along the side of her face, her skin like silk under his callused fingertips, her eyes as filled with him as his surely were with her.

"Tell me," he said gruffly. "I need to hear the words."

Isabella sighed, and what he heard in that single expulsion of breath almost stopped his heart.

"Make love to me," she said, lifting her arms,

winding them around his neck, standing on her toes so she could press herself against him. "Please," she whispered. "I want you so badly—"

Rio knew the right answer. The one logic demanded, but he was long past logic.

He said her name. Took her mouth in a deep, hungry kiss. Then he scooped her into his arms and, still kissing her, carried her swiftly through the dark, silent house.

To his bed.

CHAPTER EIGHT

THE bedroom was an ebony sea dappled by the light of an ivory moon.

Rio's bed stood beneath a star-filled skylight.

He carried Isabella to it, still kissing her, never wanting the kiss to end, and slowly, slowly let her slide down his body until she was on her feet.

"Isabella," he whispered against her lips.

"Matteo," she sighed, and he groaned because his name—and yes, it was his name—sounded so right, coming from her mouth.

He cupped her face with his hands, lifted it to his, traced the arcs of her cheeks with his thumbs.

And kissed her.

He loved kissing her.

Loved everything about it.

The feel, the sweetness of her lips. The little moans that escaped her throat.

He'd always enjoyed sex, everything about it,

from the simplicity of kissing to the hot excitement of completion, but kissing Isabella—

How could there be this much pleasure in a kiss?

She tasted of wine. Of the night. Of herself. And of desire.

For him.

Only for him.

He said her name again as he gathered her against him. She rose on tiptoe, returning kiss for kiss. He slid his hands under her sweatshirt. She cried out when he cupped her naked breasts. Her flesh was cool, the nipples pebbled.

"Oh, God," she whispered, her voice trembling, "oh, God, yes, Matteo, yes, yes."

It almost undid him.

He drew her arms up, followed the path with his hands, reached her wrists and slowly, carefully eased off her sweatshirt and dropped it to the floor. He drew her close, kissed her throat, the slope of her breast. He could feel her heart pounding beneath his lips and he ached to go further, to take her nipple into his mouth, but now her entire body was trembling; she was breathing hard and he told himself to go slowly, slowly, not to frighten her, not to do anything too quickly.

But she rose on her toes. Leaned into him. Moved against him.

"Isabella," he said roughly. "Sweetheart, when you do that—when you do that—"

He groaned, drew her to him again and kissed her, this kiss deeper, harder, and she moaned softly and gave herself up to its hot demand.

His hands dropped to her waist. She had tied the cord of the sweatpants as tightly as possible. Still, the pants were loose on her and rested lightly on her hips.

He wanted to see her.

Was it too soon?

He had to find out.

He put his thumbs under the soft cotton waistband. Isabella shook her head and burrowed against him.

"Matteo," she said, and he knew that yes, it was too soon. Instead, he wove his fingers into her hair until she raised her head and looked up at him.

She was beautiful. Real. No artifice. Just her.

Had there ever been a woman in his bed who had not done anything to enhance her looks? He didn't think so but, hell, he didn't want to think about other women now.

There was no one else.

There was only Isabella.

He kissed her. Again. And again, until he felt her relax against him. She was so warm in his arms, her naked skin like satin under his hands as he stroked her. His fingers brushed the sides of her breasts and she trembled.

"Matteo. I should have told you before this—I should have told you that I—that I haven't—" She swallowed drily and made what she knew was probably the understatement of the decade. "I haven't done this very much."

He hated the whisper of apology he heard in her voice—and hated himself for the swift, primitive response it engendered in him.

He believed firmly in sexual equality but deep in his man-as-mighty-hunter heart, he knew there was something special in being the man who would teach a woman the meaning of passion.

"I just—I just don't want you to expect—to expect—"

Rio kissed her to silence.

"All I expect is to please you," he said gruffly, and vowed to himself that he would.

Added reason to take all the time in the world to

make love to her, even as—hell, especially as the urge to back her against the wall, free himself of his sweatpants and hers and thrust into her, beat hard in his blood.

He knew he could do that, despite her admission of near-innocence. He was good at sex, and at making sex last. He liked to prolong the pleasure for himself and for the woman he was with.

He liked knowing he had such complete control of himself, of his lover, of the moment.

Tonight, all that mattered was pleasuring Isabella.

He tilted her face up to his. Kissed her mouth until her lips parted and he could feast on the sweet taste of her. Kissed her throat until she moaned and her head fell back. Kissed her breast, such a delicate breast, kissed lower, lower...

She cried out as his lips closed around one nipple. The taste of her flesh was sweeter than anything he'd ever known. He tongued it and she cried out again, the sound urgent, shocked, hot with pleasure and excitement.

His hands went to the waistband of her sweatpants again. She held her breath. *Now,* he told himself, and slowly, slowly, he eased the sweat-pants down her legs.

A groan broke from his throat as he gathered her against him and felt the warmth of her naked body against his.

Cristo, he wanted to see her.

But she was trembling, and he knew it was still too soon.

Sweat beaded his forehead. His pulse was going crazy. Still, he held her. Only held her. He could feel her heart racing against his, or maybe it was his heart racing against hers.

It didn't matter.

He waited, waited, waited until she sighed. Her hand crept up his chest, to his shoulders and she whispered his name.

He let go of her and pulled off his sweatshirt. Pushed down his bottoms. Stepped out of them.

Then he drew her into his arms again, closing his eyes at the hot, delicious feel of her against him.

"Isabella," he murmured, his arms tightening around her as he bent to her and took her lips in kiss after kiss, each deeper than the last. He lifted her against him, her breasts against his chest, her belly against his and she gasped when his aroused flesh pressed at the apex of her thighs.

"Matteo," she whispered, and he heard all the questions in the world in the way she said his name.

"It's all right, *cara*," he said gruffly.

"I don't know if—I mean, I don't know if—"

He was big. He knew that. In typical male fashion, the knowledge that a woman's eyes would widen with pleasurable anticipation when she first saw him, erect and eager, when she first felt him, naked against her, had always given his ego a boost.

Those women had not been Isabella.

"Don't be afraid," he said softly. He took her hand. Brought it to him. "This is only another part of me. I won't hurt you, sweetheart. I swear it."

He caught his breath as her fingers brushed over him. Touched him. She made a soft, questioning sound. He closed his eyes. Told himself not to do anything foolish but then she closed her hand around him and he had to grit his teeth to keep from tumbling her onto the bed.

He let her explore him. He was the one trembling now, as he fought to hang on to his sanity.

At last, he groaned. It was too much.

"Isabella," he said thickly, "sweetheart—"

Her arms wound around his neck, and he took her down to the bed. When he drew back, she grabbed for the duvet bunched beneath them. He knew she wanted to cover herself, that being undressed before a man was new to her. But he had to see her and he caught her hands, kissed them, then gently brought them to her sides.

"It's all right," he whispered. "Isabella. Let me see you."

She drew an unsteady breath. He pulled back. And looked at the woman he wanted with every hard pulse of the blood beating through his veins.

His heart turned over.

She was more than beautiful.

She was exquisite.

Small, tip-tilted breasts, crowned by delicate rose nipples. A narrow waist. A woman's hips, curved and lush. And at the juncture of her thighs, a cluster of dark curls.

He bent his head. Took one nipple and then the

other into the heat of his mouth. She moaned; her fingers threaded through his hair.

"Matteo," she whispered, "oh, Matteo—"

He moved between her thighs. Kissed her eyes. Her mouth. Her throat. Her breasts. He moved lower. Lower still. Her belly. Her navel. The dark curls at the juncture of her thighs.

Her breath caught.

"Wait! You can't—"

He could. Nothing would stop him. He wanted to inhale her scent, taste the sweetness of her most intimate flesh.

Rio put his face against her. Found her, licked her and she gave a long cry of rapture that rose into the night.

"Oh, God," she sobbed, "oh, God…"

Her thighs fell open. He slipped his hands beneath her, lifted her to him, kissed her until she was weeping. He moved up her body, took her mouth in a long, deep kiss, let her taste their mingled passion on his tongue.

"Matteo," she sobbed. "Please. Please—"

He could wait no longer.

Blindly, he pulled open the drawer in the nightstand. His hands were shaking; it took an eternity to tear open the little packet, then ease the condom along his length.

He felt her eyes on him.

That she was watching him made him harder than ever—except, that wasn't possible. Any harder, he would die, he thought, and he came back to her, whispered her name, knelt between her still-parted thighs.

And paused at the entrance to her body.

Rio shuddered.

The sensation was exquisite.

And he, the man who knew how to make sex last, knew he was dangerously close to the edge.

She was wet. Hot. Tight. He moved slowly. Deliberately. It was exquisite torture. Holding back. Watching her face. Seeing her eyes blur, her lips part.

Feeling her ready to take him inside her.

Cristo, it was too much, too much, too much—

Her arms tightened around him. She lifted her hips.

"Don't," he said. "When you do that, I can't—I can't—" She moved again, brought his mouth to hers and kissed him.

Rio closed his eyes and sank into her.

She gave a little sob.

"Did I hurt you?" he whispered.

She answered by lifting her hips again. And again. Until he was groaning, holding her against him, moving inside her, faster, harder, harder…

Isabella screamed with pleasure.

And Rio threw back his head and flew with her into the night.

Time passed.

Rio's face was buried against Isabella's throat. The delicious smell of her—woman, soap, sex— was in every breath he took.

It was the most alluring scent he'd ever known.

And, *Dio,* he was going to crush her if he didn't move. But when she felt him start to shift his weight, she tightened her arms around him.

"No," she whispered. "Stay with me, please."

"I'm not going anywhere, sweetheart. I'm just afraid I'm too heavy for you."

"You're not. I just—I just want—"

He rolled to his side without letting go of her, tucked her against him, his arms holding her fast.

"Me, too," he said gruffly, and kissed her mouth.

She sighed; the soft sound, the whisper of her breath, filled him with pleasure. "You okay?"

She nodded. Her hair slid over his skin like silk.

"Are you sure? I didn't mean to go so fast—"

Isabella put her fingers lightly across his lips.

"You were wonderful."

"Yeah?" He smiled. "Not that I'm looking for compliments—" She gave a soft laugh and he brushed his mouth over hers. "You're what's wonderful, *cara.*"

"You're making me blush."

Rio grinned, propped his head on his hand and looked down at her. It was true. Her face, kissed by starlight, had turned a soft shade of pink.

"I know it's silly, after—after we just had—"

"After we just made love," he said, his voice rough.

She nodded, traced the lines of his face with her fingertip.

"You have a scar on your chin."

"Uh-huh," he said, sucking her finger into the heat of his mouth.

"How did it happen?"

He shrugged. "I do some boxing. Not professionally," he added quickly, when her eyes widened. "Just to work out."

"It's very sexy."

He grinned. "So is the way you blush."

She smiled up at him. It made him want to kiss her again. Make love to her again. Bring her to the edge of the universe and hold her there before letting go.

Great.

His thoughts were turning him hard. An out-of-control lover. Just what she didn't need.

But he couldn't resist giving her one more kiss. And then another. And another...

She moved against him.

He groaned, leaned his forehead against hers. "No. It's too soon—"

Her hand slipped between them. "Is it?" she said in tones of absolute innocence.

Cristo, she was teasing him. And he loved it.

Another little packet. Another condom. Then he gave a low growl and drew her to him, brought her leg high over his hip and slid into her.

Isabella moaned. Kissed him. Bit lightly into his lip.

This time, he set a harder rhythm. She met

it, matched it, and he caught her by the waist, brought her on top of him, watched her face, her eyes as she rode him.

At the end, she collapsed against him.

They fell asleep that way, her body covering his, his arms holding her tight.

Isabella came awake with a start.

She was in a strange room. A room swathed in darkness save for a sliver of light at the far end.

Her heart leaped into her throat.

The sliver of light grew. It was from a door, and the door was opening to reveal a tall, dark figure…

"Isabella?"

The breath whooshed from her lungs.

"Matteo," she said in a shaky whisper.

Of course. She was in Rio D'Aquila's house, in Matteo Rossi's bed.

"Sweetheart. Did I startle you?"

She sat up, holding the duvet to her throat.

"What time is it?"

Matteo came to the bed, made quick work of the duvet she held and drew her into his arms. God, the feel of his skin against hers…

"It's four-something in the morning." He pressed a kiss into her hair. "Forgive me, *cara*. I didn't mean to wake you."

He smelled wonderful. Man and sex. And, of course, Matteo. She thought of how his skin would taste if she nipped his shoulder, of what he would do if she put her hands on his chest and pushed him down backward on the bed.

"Hey." He reached for a long ebony curl, let it wind around his finger and gave a gentle tug. "What are you thinking about?"

Isabella cleared her throat. "Just that—that it's fine that I'm awake. I have to get up anyway."

"Ah," he said matter-of-factly. "Sure. Let me get you my robe. The bathroom is chill—"

"No. I mean, it's time I got up."

"It is?"

She nodded.

He put a finger under her chin and tilted her face up.

"Why?"

"Well, because—because—"

She frowned.

It was a good question. She'd made love with this man. Twice. She had slept with him, literally.

Draped over him—she remembered that—naked skin to naked skin. And she was going to leave his bed because it was four in the morning and instead of making love, they were having a conversation?

Why, indeed? she thought again…

And giggled.

"Isabella Orsini," Matteo said sternly. Gently, he pushed her back on the bed and came down above her. "Are you laughing?"

She shook her head. "No," she gasped, and giggled again.

"Laughter. Just what a man wants to hear after he's made love to a woman."

"I wasn't—"

"You were." His tone softened; a devilish grin lifted the corners of his lips. "I'm glad."

Isabella smiled.

"So am I. This was—"

"Indeed it was," he said solemnly, but he spoiled it with another quick grin.

She smiled. "I don't know if I can move."

"Good. I don't want you to move. Well, not for a little while, anyway."

Sighing, she wrapped her arms around him.

Crazy, he knew, but that she wanted his weight on her like this made him happy.

"Matteo?"

"Mmm?"

Isabella put her hand against his jaw. His skin was bristly with early morning stubble. It felt masculine and sexy, and she thought of how wonderful it would feel against her breasts.

"Of all the things I ever thought about—about sex—"

"About making love," he said quietly.

She nodded. "I never imagined feeling so, well, so happy afterward."

Her words, her simple honesty, made his heart swell. He turned on his side, gathered her against him and pressed a kiss into her hair.

The thing was, he'd never imagined feeling like this after sex, either. Sated? Sure. Relaxed? Of course. Content? Yes, absolutely.

But happy, to use her word…

Not like this.

And *happy* was the wrong word. What he felt was bigger than that, deeper, more intense.

Much more intense, he thought, and he gave her a quick kiss and sat up.

"Okay," he said briskly. "Here's the schedule."

"Oh, God." Isabella gave a dramatic sigh. "I *hate* schedules!"

He grinned. "Now, why does that not surprise me?"

"See, I like the part where you draw up the schedule." She sat up, too, wrapped her arms around him from the back and sighed. "It's the carrying out part I'm not good at."

A moment ago, establishing emotional distance had seemed important. Now, turning around, taking Isabella in his arms and smiling at her was what mattered.

"Really," he said, widening his eyes.

"You laugh, but something always goes wrong. Like yesterday. The traffic. The directions. The car. And then, poof, so much for my schedule. It went up in smoke." She smiled. "But if it hadn't, would I have met you?"

Damned right you would have, he thought.

Hell.

He had to tell her.

Soon.

But first…

First, he thought, looking at her tousled curls, her kiss-swollen mouth, first there was that schedule.

Showering together.

Breakfasting together.

Going back to bed together.

"Isabella," he said thickly, and he brought her down beneath him and forgot everything but the woman in his arms.

Forget everything, including a condom.

Dawn was tinting the sky crimson.

Rio awoke alone in his bed. He could hear the shower running.

Isabella, he thought, smiling—

And then his smile faded as he remembered that he hadn't used a condom the last time they'd made love.

Cristo.

He had never been that careless before. He always used protection, even when a woman said she was on the Pill. Only a fool took chances. He knew the possibility that Isabella might become pregnant was small. Miniscule, really. One ejaculation? Things didn't happen that way. He knew couples who'd tried for years to conceive.

Still, he would mention it to her.

Ask if this was her so-called safe time of the month. Tell her that, of course, if anything happened, he would—he would help her with whatever had to be done.

It was a sobering thought.

Even more sobering was the fact that he hadn't remembered to use a condom.

That his naive, inexperienced Isabella had driven every logical thought from his head.

No woman had ever done that before.

His smile wavered.

He wasn't sure he liked the feeling.

The sound of the shower stopped. Rio sat up, swung his feet to the floor, went to the bathroom and quietly pushed open the door. His lover stood before the mirror. She'd knotted a bath towel around her like a sarong; she was using another to dry her hair.

Botticelli, he thought, Venus, rising from the sea—and, all at once, nothing mattered as much as coming up behind her and wrapping his arms around her waist.

She smiled at him in the mirror. "Hello," she said softly.

Rio drew her back against him. "Isabella," he whispered.

It seemed all he was capable of saying and when she sighed his name—*Matteo*—he thought, once again, how right his name, his true name, sounded on her lips.

She was Isabella. He was Matteo. Two strangers, brought together by chance.

And now, they were lovers.

Lovers.

Something swept through him. An emotion that had nothing to do with sexual pleasure and everything to do with—with—

With what? *Dio,* he had no answers for anything.

Except for this.

"I have an idea," he said.

She smiled. "I can tell."

He laughed.

"That, too. But I have another idea."

Isabella turned in his arms, placed her hands against his chest, looked up at him.

"What?"

"Don't go back to the city. Not just yet."

"But I have to. I—"

"Stay with me." He bent to her, brushed his lips over hers. "I want to show you something."

She touched her fingers to his lips.

"What is it?"

"A place. One that's all mine."

She smiled. "And where is this place?"

"You'll see."

"Ah. A secret."

"One I want to share only with you. Spend the weekend with me, *cara*. Please."

Isabella thought of all the reasons to say no.

It was Saturday, and she always worked the Union Square Outdoor Market on Saturday. Initially, she'd sold bouquets and plants; now, increasingly, she sold more elaborate flower arrangements. It was excellent and inexpensive advertising for her business.

There was more, too.

She did her weekly food shopping Saturdays: staples at Costco, fresh stuff at—naturally—the Union Square market and at Whole Foods. Plus, she was supposed to meet Anna for lunch and—oh, hell—return her car. Okay. That was another story altogether.

"Isabella," Matteo said, "stay with me."

The towel fell away as she went up on her toes and gave him her answer with a kiss.

CHAPTER NINE

A LITTLE after dawn, Isabella announced it was time for breakfast, and that she would prepare it.

"Not to boast or anything," she said, fluttering her lashes, "but I make the world's best scrambled eggs. And bacon. And toast. And coffee."

When Rio said he'd help, she pointed to a kitchen chair and said, "Sit."

He laughed.

He couldn't remember the last time someone had told him what to do, even in a teasing way. He could just picture the looks on the faces of his staff if anyone had.

But this wasn't anyone, it was Isabella.

And he certainly couldn't recall a woman making him breakfast. Not that women didn't offer. He simply never took them up on it. There was something far too intimate in letting a woman cook your breakfast, even if she'd spent the night in your bed.

Sex was one thing.

Breakfast was another.

It was the kind of logic only another man could understand.

In fact, he'd once had that conversation with Dante Orsini, when Dante was still a bachelor.

They'd bumped into each other at a Starbucks a little past eight one morning, Dante paying for a *caffè Americano* just as Rio ordered a *caffè Macchiato.*

For some reason, they'd exchanged slightly embarrassed looks.

Dante had spoken first.

"I, ah, I didn't have time for coffee at home this morning," he'd said.

"Me, neither," Rio had said, his tone as uncomfortable as Dante's. Then he'd laughed a little shamefacedly and admitted that the problem was a woman who'd wanted to make coffee for him, and Dante had grinned and admitted to the same thing.

"Too much togetherness," Rio had said. "Last thing I want to face in the morning is a woman hell-bent on showing me her domestic side."

Dante had grinned and agreed.

Talk about your own words coming back to haunt you, Rio thought. What would Dante say right about now, if he knew his relative was in this kitchen, doing exactly that?

It was not a good thing to dwell on.

"Matteo." Rio blinked. Isabella, arms folded, gave a dramatic sigh. "I don't see you sitting down and leaving this to me."

He grinned.

"Yes, ma'am," he said, and then he grabbed her, lifted her off her feet and kissed her.

Then he sat down and hoped he was remembering correctly, and that there actually were bacon and eggs in the refrigerator.

There were. Free-range eggs, Isabella said with approval, and explained why hens should be kept cage-free. There was bacon, too, from—he lost track of the "from" part, but Isabella pronounced it perfect.

She was what was perfect, Rio thought.

And made a mental note to thank his caretaker for laying in the right foods.

He'd have to thank the guy for a lot of things, starting with leaving before Isabella arrived yesterday.

Was it only yesterday?

It seemed impossible that he'd only known her so short a time. He felt as if he'd known her for a lifetime. He was so at ease with her, so relaxed.

He couldn't remember feeling this way with another woman.

With anyone.

No pressures. No demands. No trying to read the true meaning behind her words or actions.

She was with him because she wanted to be with him, not because of who he was or what he might be able to do for her. He couldn't recall that ever happening. Everybody wanted something from him. It was part of his life and though he hated it, he'd learned to endure it.

Nothing about yesterday, last night or this morning had anything to do with endurance… Except in bed, he thought, biting back a smile. Not that he'd ever had any complaints but, *Cristo,* there wasn't an eighteen-year-old out there who could possibly have anything on him today.

And it was Isabella's doing.

The cold truth was that a woman who said "no" to a man's sexual advances often became a prize to pursue. The even colder truth was that once a man captured that prize, his interest lessened.

Nothing even close to that was happening to him.

The more he made love to Isabella, the more he wanted her. And it wasn't because she was so innocent that every touch, every caress brought her such unabashed delight and surprise.

It was because making love to her, with her, had a power that went beyond the physical. He couldn't explain it to himself except to suspect it had to do with, well, with friendship. He liked being with her, outside of bed as well as in it.

His life in what he increasingly thought of as the real world was a full, successful one. He liked who he was, his achievements, the complexities of business…

But now—now, he had the sense that something had been missing from it. A day didn't have to begin and end with appointments and conferences, it could begin and end with a woman.

With this woman.

Rio frowned.

Not that he could imagine his life centering on her. On any woman, but—

"—or runny?"

Rio blinked. Isabella was looking at him, her winged eyebrows arched, waiting for an answer to a question he hadn't heard.

"Sorry, *cara*. What did you ask me?"

"I asked if you like your eggs well-cooked or runny?"

"Runny," he said with dignity, "is not a word meant to pique the appetite."

She grinned. She had an extraordinary grin, one that involved her nose wrinkling with delight.

"Okay, I'll rephrase that. Soft or hard?"

It was his turn to grin.

"I can think of a lot of answers to that question but none that have to do with scrambling eggs."

"Keep your mind on eggs," she said with mock severity, "unless you want us both to die of hunger."

She was right. They'd eaten hardly anything last night. Rio gave a sigh suited to a long-suffering male in torment.

"Soft," he said.

"Good. Because—"

"But definitely not runny. And while you're

asking, I like my bacon crisp, my toast light, my coffee black—"

She poked out her tongue. He grinned again.

"Is that a no? Or is it an invitation?"

She blushed. He loved it when she did but for all those charming blushes, he could see her becoming more and more relaxed with him.

She'd begun touching him more. Exploring him, during sex. She was more comfortable with him in other ways, too. What she'd just done, for instance, giving him little teasing answers to his questions.

He had the feeling she'd learned to keep herself quietly in the background most of her life.

But not with him.

She'd been feisty from the second she'd come limping up his driveway.

Now, she was giving him orders.

And she was sexy as hell.

He wanted to know more about her. He wanted to know *all* about her. He usually made a point of avoiding learning more than necessary about his lovers. Where they came from, what they wanted out of life… He knew it might seem—that word again—cold not to show an interest.

It wasn't. It was just that those things were too personal.

A man and woman didn't have to open themselves to each other's scrutiny just because they slept together.

Now, watching Isabella beating eggs hard enough so every part of her was jiggling—and, *Dio,* those jiggled parts were distracting—he realized he didn't feel that way this time.

He wanted to know everything about Isabella. Everything, from her favorite books to her favorite foods. What she'd been like as a little girl, although he knew she had to have been bright and sweet and adorable. How she'd come to love working with her hands in the soil.

Most of all, he wondered why sex was so new to her.

Male chauvinist bastard that he was, he loved sensing that he was the first man to make her cry out when he brought her to the brink of orgasm and held her there, suspended, until neither she nor he could wait another heartbeat for the incredible pleasure of release.

They'd come close to not even making it out of the bedroom a little while ago.

Each time she'd tried to get dressed, he'd grabbed the top or bottom of the sweat suit and demanded ransom in the form of a kiss. He'd finally relented, or so he'd allowed her to think, letting her put on the bottoms before he danced away with the top.

Isabella had narrowed her eyes and slapped her hands on her hips. It had made for a delectable sight, the pants riding low, her lovely breasts naked, the pink nipples delicately peaked.

"I cannot get dressed if you keep undressing me," she'd said with an indignation that didn't match the laughter in her eyes. "And you did say you wanted an early start to take me to this secret place you absolutely refuse to talk about!"

He'd grabbed her, bent her back over his arm for a dramatic kiss, told her fine, she could banish him now.

"But just think of what you'll be missing," he'd said, curving his hand around one sweet breast and putting his mouth to the tip.

She'd moaned—*Dio,* he loved that moan of hers—but then she'd turned the table on him, putting her lips to his ear and whispering, "You think of what *you'll* be missing, too," and the sexy taunt

had made him so hard he'd kissed her mouth—
and gotten the hell out of there before he tumbled
her back on the bed again.

He damned well wanted to. But there wasn't
time.

Isabella didn't know it yet, but they had several
hours of flying time ahead of them.

So he'd gone downstairs, into the freshness of
the morning where he'd listened to the heartbeat
of the ocean while he breathed deep and got his
hormones under control.

Then he'd phoned the Plaza and left a message
for a visiting Greek ship owner, canceling an appointment for drinks that evening. He gave it a
couple of minutes and then he made another call,
this time to his office where he left voice mail for
his PA to pick up on Monday.

"I won't be in today, Jeanne. Reschedule my
appointments for the middle of the week."

Jeanne would be shocked.

Well, so was he.

He never canceled appointments, much less
cleared his entire calendar, but then, he'd never
been—he'd never been eager to spend time alone
with a woman before.

If things went as he intended, he and Isabella would still be in Mustique come Monday and Tuesday and, for all he knew, Wednesday.

Mustique.

A beautiful little island in the Caribbean. That was his surprise; that was where he was taking her. It was a long flight but worth it.

He was certain she would love the villa he owned there.

Rio sat back in his chair, feet crossed at the ankles, arms folded, watching Isabella bustle around the kitchen in his sweat suit.

She looked spectacular in it but he suspected he'd have to do a lot of fast-talking to convince her to go on wearing it while he flew them to the island.

There wasn't much choice.

It was early. Just after 6:00 a.m. The village boutiques wouldn't be open yet. They *would* open, he was certain, for Rio D'Aquila, but that wasn't who he was.

He was Matteo Rossi.

And until the moment was right, that's who he would remain.

As for the villa—he'd bought it with part of his

first big chunk of money. Five million dollars, more money than he'd imagined existed in the entire world.

His lawyer had invited him to celebrate by flying down to what he'd called his hideaway in the Caribbean for the weekend. That "hideaway" had turned out to be Mustique.

Gentle green hills. A pure blue sea. White sand beaches. And best of all, the attorney said, privacy.

Mustique, privately owned, was a getaway destination for lots of rich, famous people. There was no guarantee a reporter or photographer wouldn't leap out of a shrub, but if you were careful, the odds were good no one would point a finger and say, "Ohmygod, look who that is!"

Rio, who hadn't been famous back then, couldn't imagine needing a place like that but the beauty, the quiet of the island had enthralled him. His lawyer had turned him on to a small villa with a private stretch of beach that was going at a bargain price, thanks to some unfortunate soul's bankruptcy. Rio had taken a deep breath and bought it.

A couple of years later, he'd legally changed his

name from Matteo Rossi to Rio D'Aquila. Everything he now owned—his Manhattan condo, the place in Southampton, his homes abroad, his Brazilian estate—were Rio's.

For some reason, he'd left the deed to the villa untouched. Matteo Rossi, not Rio D'Aquila, owned it.

One less lie to deal with today, he thought, and despite Isabella's command that he sit, he rose, went to the stove, put his arms around her, nuzzled aside her dark curls and kissed the nape of her neck.

"Careful or the bacon will burn," she said, but she turned in his embrace and kissed him.

It was a long, deep kiss. It made him want her. Again. He hardened against her and she gave one of those sexy little moans he'd come to love, but then she put her hands against his chest and said, with a breathless little laugh, that he was better than any of the diets she'd ever tried when it came to keeping down the daily calorie count.

"Why would you need a diet?" he said with absolute truthfulness. One of the things he lov—he liked about her was that she didn't look like a toothpick.

"Flattery," she said, "will get you a burned breakfast."

He laughed. She grinned, her nose doing that cute wrinkly thing, gave him another quick kiss, and he went back to the table, swung a chair around so he could sit on it and watch her some more, his arms folded along the back, his chin propped on his folded arms.

She was going to love the villa.

He hadn't been there in a long time. He'd been too busy, making deals and making money. A housekeeper and groundskeeper came by every couple of weeks to keep things organized.

And he'd never taken a woman there.

That was another good thing. A very good thing. Mustique would be about fresh starts. And honesty.

It would also be about being in a place where he could take Isabella out to some small, intimate café for dinner. Hold her in his arms as they moved to slow music on a tiny dance floor. Behave like real people. And any time, in the cool of the house or the heat of the sun, they could go into each other's arms and make love.

And then...

A muscle flickered in Rio's jaw.

Then, when the time was right, he'd admit everything. That he had not been—not been completely forthright with her but then, this had begun as a clever game.

How could he possibly have known it would turn into something else?

Isabella, his Isabella, would understand. He was certain of it. She wasn't a prima donna. Okay, she might be a little miffed at first but once she got over the shock, she'd laugh along with him at how he'd dug the hole he'd made for himself deeper and deeper.

She would, wouldn't she?

Wouldn't she?

"What a long face!"

Rio jumped. Isabella was standing beside him, smiling.

"A long face, and *before* you've tasted my cooking!"

She had two plates in her hands. Rio shot to his feet and took them from her. He smiled, leaned in and kissed the tip of her nose.

"Everything looks perfect," he said.

Perfect eggs, perfect bacon, perfect toast…

Perfect woman, he thought, and his heart did something it had never done before.

It soared.

They were almost at the airport when he told her what his "surprise" was.

Isabella looked at him as if he'd lost his mind.

"We're flying to where?"

"Mustique. It's an island—"

"—in the Caribbean. I get that. But—but I can't just—just do something so—so outrageous on the spur of the moment!"

"That's what doing things on the spur of the moment is all about," Rio said, steering around a pickup truck loaded with crates of lettuce. "If it's not outrageous, what's the point?"

She stared at him. There was truth in that, if you were into doing outrageous things, but—

"But?" he said, and flashed her a smile. "I can hear the *but* from here, sweetheart."

"But," she said, "I can't."

"Because?"

"Well, because—because I have commitments."

"What commitments?"

What, indeed? Or maybe the question was, what

commitment could possibly supercede the sheer joy of flying to an island in the sun with her lover? Her gorgeous, sexy, amazing lover.

"Well—well, I'm supposed to have lunch with Anna."

Rio reached into the pocket of his blue chambray shirt, took out his cell phone and handed it to her.

"Call her. Tell her you can't make it."

"I'm supposed to return her—" Isabella sucked in her breath. "Oh, boy. I'm supposed to return her car."

"Ah. The car. Right. I almost forgot that. Where'd you have the accident? Can you give me some kind of location?"

"No, not really. I just… Wait. There was a field of corn on my right."

Based on what he knew of the area, that narrowed things down to something like a zillion square miles.

"How about some visual clue? A house. A store. A sign."

"A sign," she said eagerly. "I passed it maybe five minutes before the car drove off the road."

"Uh-huh," Rio said, trying not to laugh. "Can you remember what it said?"

She frowned. "A man's name. James. Jack. Jeffrey." She snapped her fingers. "Jonas," she said happily. "Jonas's Organic Vegetables."

"Excellent. Call Anna, then give me the phone. I'll call—" He'd almost said he'd call his caretaker. "I'll call a service station and arrange to have the car towed."

"But Anna—"

Rio checked his mirrors and pulled his truck onto the shoulder of the road. He undid his seat belt, reached over, cupped Isabella's face with his hands and gave her a long, deep kiss.

"I want us to be alone," he said gruffly. "In a place that's entirely mine." He stroked a curl from her temple. "If that's what you want, call your sister. If it isn't—" He took a deep breath. "If it isn't, I'll drive you back to the city, right now."

Isabella could feel her pulse racing.

This was crazy.

All of it.

And she didn't do crazy things.

She was not the driven-to-succeed type like Anna. She was not a walk-the-tightrope-over-the-chasm daredevil like her brothers. She was—she was Izzy, who liked to plant things and watch them grow. She was steady and nurturing.

Except, she wasn't only that Izzy anymore.

She was also Isabella, a woman sexually and emotionally awakened. A woman who had found a man who made her heartbeat rise into the stratosphere. Life had handed her a gift. It was something that probably would never come her way again.

"Isabella?" Matteo, her wonderful lover, looked deep into her eyes. "Am I taking you to the city, or to Mustique?"

Isabella took a steadying breath and punched Anna's number into the cell phone.

One ring. Two. Four and then, at last, Anna's voice, husky with sleep.

"Hello?"

"Anna. It's me. Izzy."

"Izzy? What time is it?" Anna's voice sharpened. Isabella could picture her getting a look at the clock, then sitting upright in bed. "Are you okay?"

"I'm fine. I just—I just called to tell you I can't meet you for lunch."

"Why not?" A pause, and then Anna's voice hardened. "Isabella. Something's wrong. I can tell."

"Nothing's wrong. Why should anything be wrong? I told you, I can't—"

There was mumbling in the background. Isabella rolled her eyes. Wonderful. Anna's husband, Draco, was awake now, too.

"No," Anna said, "it's just Izzy."

It's just Izzy. Isabella reached across the truck's console and felt Matteo's warm, strong hand clasp hers.

"Also," she said, "I wrecked your car."

"Ohmygod! Izzy! You're not all right! You're in the hospital. Where? I can be there in—"

"Anna," Isabella said, "will you listen to me? The car's a mess. I'm fine."

"Not fine," Matteo said softly, lifting her hand to his lips. "You're perfect."

"Izzy? Who is that? You're with someone. A man? Izzy? Are you with a—"

"I am," Isabella said, her breath catching as Matteo sucked her finger into the heat of his mouth. "I am with a man. I've been with him since yesterday. And I'm going to spend the weekend—"

"The week," Matteo murmured. To hell with returning to the city by Wednesday.

"And I'm going to spend the week with him."

Silence. Then she could hear Anna drag in a deep breath.

"Iz. Remember when I phoned you from Rome that time? And I asked you if you remember Psych 101, that stuff about fantasizing sex with a stranger?"

Isabella looked at her lover. She held up a finger, opened the door and stepped onto the grass.

"I do, indeed," she said calmly.

"Remember the rest of what you said?" Anna's voice rose. "About fantasizing sex with a stranger? A dark and dangerous stranger? You warned me against it. *You warned me!*"

"And you really listened," Isabella said with saccharine sweetness.

"Isabella. Damnit, when did you meet this man? Where? What do you know about him? For God's sake, Iz—"

"When did you meet Draco? What did you know about him? As I recall, you fell into bed with him, what, a couple of hours after you set eyes on each other."

"I am not going to discuss that with you," Anna said coldly. "Besides, that was different."

Isabella laughed. "Really?"

"Of course! I knew what I was doing. I had some experience dealing with men." Anna's tone softened. "This could be an awful mistake, Iz. Do you realize that?"

Isabella hesitated. She looked into the truck, at Matteo. His eyebrows rose. Did she need him with her? he was asking.

Yes, she thought, *oh, yes.*

"Izzy? Did you hear what I said? This could be a terrible, terrible mistake!"

Isabella shot her lover a reassuring smile. Then she turned away from him again.

"It could be," she said quietly. "I know that. But I'm happy, Anna. I've never been so happy before."

"Oh, Izzy! Honey, I want you to be happy, but—"

"Isabella?"

Matteo had gotten out of the truck, He came to Isabella and held out his hand. Isabella's heart lifted. She smiled and put her hand in his.

"Anna. I have to go. We're flying to—to—" She looked at Matteo, who leaned down and kissed her.

"Mustique," he said softly, and kissed her again.

"Mustique," Isabella said.

"Mustique?" Anna shrieked. "That's halfway around the world!"

"It's in the Caribbean."

"Jeez, Izzy, I know that! I only meant—" A long breath; Draco's low voice saying something. "Yes. Right. Iz? At least tell me who this man is. What's his name? How did you meet him? What does he do?"

"His name is Matteo Rossi. I met him at Rio D'Aquila's estate in Southampton. Matteo is the caretaker."

"And a pilot," Matteo said, with a smile.

"And a pilot," Isabella added, her eyes widening.

"The caretaker?" Anna said. "Ohmygod, Iz, this is a bad remake of *Lady Chatterley's Lover!*"

Isabella laughed. "Wrong," she said. "It's an excellent remake."

Then she closed the phone, gave it back to Matteo and when he kissed her this time, she knew she hadn't told Anna the most important thing of all.

She was more than happy.

She was in love.

CHAPTER TEN

Isabella had flown before.

Her brothers owned a sleek, private jet. She'd been up in it, of course. And she'd flown in commercial jets. Not often, but a few times.

This was different.

She was in the copilot's seat of a handsome plane Matteo said was a prop-jet.

And the man beside her, the pilot, was her lover.

She hadn't had time to think about that for very long. They'd parked at the airport, gone into a small building, Matteo had talked with a pleasant man behind a desk, and then he'd led her to a plane tethered near the runway.

"Does the plane belong to Rio D'Aquila?" she'd asked.

"It's mine," Matteo had answered, and then he'd quickly corrected himself. "I mean, I feel as if it's mine."

"Because you're the one who flies it?"

"Yes," he said, running a hand lightly over the fuselage. "But D'Aquila pilots it, too."

"Not as well as you, I bet."

Matteo had turned to her and ruffled her hair.

"Actually, he's pretty good."

"He doesn't mind that we're using it? Well, I mean, he doesn't know about me, but—"

"He doesn't mind," Matteo had said a little brusquely. "I wouldn't do this if I thought he would."

Isabella had put her hand on his arm.

"No," she'd said softly, "of course you wouldn't." She'd paused. "You really like him."

"I like some things about him. Other things… Yeah. There are things about him that definitely need changing. Basically, he's just a man, you know? He isn't all good or all bad."

He'd kissed her, a quick kiss, and then he'd become all purpose and efficiency as he made his way around the plane for what he'd called an inspection.

"Okay," he'd finally said.

He'd held out his hand, the same as he had at the truck, and Isabella had taken it and stepped into the sleek aircraft. He'd motioned her into a seat in the cockpit, told her to buckle herself in. Then he'd checked to make sure her seat belt was tight; he'd buckled himself in, too, put on a set of headphones, reached for what looked like a sea of dials and knobs and controls that had to be scrutinized to complete what he explained was a preflight checklist.

Isabella watched him. What an amazing man he was, capable of doing such varied things.

"I've never known anybody who knew how to fly," she said. "I mean, it's such an unusual thing to do—"

"I loved planes from the time I was just a kid, so when I had the chance to learn, I jumped at it." He glanced at her, warmed by the interest he saw in her expression. "I was a roughneck—a guy who's part of the drilling crew—on an oil field in Brazil. The foreman had a small plane." That all-business mask slipped just enough for him to turn to her and flash a boyish grin. "I probably made an ass of myself, hanging around, asking questions, and finally he figured the only way to get rid of me was to take me up and teach me."

Isabella smiled. "You make going after what you want sound easy."

"Nothing really important is ever easy to come by." Rio's smile tilted. "But some things are worth the cost." He leaned over and kissed her. Then he shot her another of those fantastic grins. "Sit back, sweetheart, and enjoy the view."

She knew he meant the view of the earth, slipping beneath them. But what her eyes feasted on was her lover.

Her lover was relaxed, obviously very much in command, pointing out things to her, his voice taking on quiet authority when he spoke with the various air traffic controllers along their flight path.

If Anna saw him now, Isabella suddenly thought, she wouldn't have called him a caretaker with such derision.

Okay. Not derision. Anna wasn't a snob. Had Isabella said the man she was going away with was a lawyer or an accountant or a doctor, Anna would still have warned her against it, but would her voice have climbed the scales?

"Your sister wasn't happy."

Isabella stared at Matteo. "Don't tell me you read minds, too." She sighed. "No. She wasn't."

"I understand that." He looked at her, took

her hand and brought it to his lips. "She worries about you."

"Uh-huh. Anna's just a little more than a year older than I am but there are times you'd think she was my mother." She looked at him and grinned. "I already have a mother. Honestly, why would I want two?"

"So you have a sister and four brothers. A big family."

"Did I tell you all that?" She shook her head. "I talk too much."

"You don't," Rio said quickly, silently cursing himself for that slip of the tongue, "I'm just envious, is all."

"No brothers or sisters?"

"No family," he said. "I grew up in an orphanage." Hell, what was he doing? He was telling her things he'd never told anyone else. Working as a roughneck, learning to fly, now this.

"Oh." Her voice was soft. "I'm sorry."

"Don't be," he said briskly. "Life is what it is, isn't that what people say?"

"Yes. But to have nobody—"

I have you.

The words were on the tip of his tongue. That

they were, terrified him. He didn't have her. He didn't have anyone, didn't need anyone, didn't want anyone…

A voice crackled in his headset. They were coming up on an airport in the Carolinas, where he'd planned to touch down, refuel, and have a quick lunch.

Grazie Cristo for interruptions, Rio thought, and busied himself with the controls.

He tried to keep the conversation light once they were airborne again.

What had drawn Isabella to gardening?

A simple question, but she gave him an answer that made him see her as a little girl, growing up in a big house with a father she'd started out worshipping and ended up despising.

"An old country despot?" Rio said.

She shook her head.

"A crook," she said, so softly he had to strain his ears to hear her. "A *don*. A godfather. You know what that is?"

He knew, all right. How could you grow up in Italy without knowing? It occurred to him now that he'd seen the name *Cesare Orsini* in the papers, heard it on the news, never in a good way.

He'd just never associated that Orsini with his friend Dante.

Dio, how hard it must have been for Isabella, growing up with that kind of ugly notoriety. It would have been difficult enough for the Orsini brothers, but for a daughter…

"My brothers broke with our father when they were still in their teens. It was harder for Anna and me. Girls, especially good Italian girls, aren't supposed to tell their father to go to hell."

"Cara." Rio reached for her hand. "I'm so sorry you had to go through something like that."

"No. It was all right. It made us strong. You know, pretending, for our mother's sake, that we were blind to the truth…" Her tone lifted; she gave a little laugh. "And we got even. Anna became a lawyer. A damned good one. I can still remember our father saying now he'd have a consigliere of his very own and Anna looking him in the eye and saying she'd sooner represent the Borgias than him."

Rio grinned. "I like your sister already." He looked at her. "And you? What was your act of rebellion, *bella?* Wait. Don't tell me. You wanted to nurture things, which is the very opposite of what your father does in his world. And, maybe, to get your hands dirty literally, not figuratively."

"Wow." Isabella smiled. "Now you're going to tell me you're a shrink and a philosopher, along with everything else."

"I am a lot of things," Rio said, after a few seconds. "Some good. Some bad. The more you get to know me, the more you'll see that." Another pause, and then he cleared his throat. "What I hope is—is that you'll believe that the good outweighs the bad. That you will—that you will care for me—"

"I will always care for you," Isabella whispered.

And, just as suddenly as that, Rio saw the truth.

He had fallen in love with her.

The realization stunned him.

He was not a man who had ever looked for love. He was not a man who believed in love. How could this have happened? Because, like it or not, it *had* happened. He didn't doubt his feelings, not for a minute. He was in love—deeply in love—with a woman who thought he was a man he was not.

Tell her. Tell her. Tell her...

"Your turn."

Rio swung his head toward her. "My turn?"

"To tell me more about yourself."

But it wasn't. Not when they were thousands of feet above the earth. When he told her the extent of the lie he was living, the lie he'd involved her in, he wanted to be able to take her in his arms, kiss her, make her see that it wasn't important if he called himself Rio or Matteo because they were the same man.

"I want to know more about that little boy in the orphanage," she said softly. "And how he grew up to be you."

Rio nodded. He could surely tell her that. If anything, she could look back on this conversation when the time came and see that he had never lied to her about the things that mattered.

Yes, he thought. He would tell her about that little boy, and the man he'd become.

It was a story he'd never before revealed to anyone.

He told her about living on the streets of Naples after he ran away from the orphanage. He told her the truth of it, not some sanitized version. The petty thefts. The pockets he'd picked. The cars he'd broken into so he could steal things left in them.

He told her without excuses, without emotion, and though her hand tightened on his, she never interrupted, never offered stupid platitudes, and he loved her all the more for it—but the more he talked, the more he wondered if he were making a mistake.

How would she look at him, once she knew all the sordid details of his early years? But it was too late to stop. She had the right to know everything about Matteo Rossi, and why and how he had become Rio D'Aquila.

He took a deep breath.

"I had a run-in with the *polizia* right around the time I turned seventeen. I got off easy but I knew everything would change once I turned eighteen. So I stowed away on a freighter and ended up in Brazil. I was broke and scared. There must have been a hundred times I thought about getting back on another freighter and heading home."

"But you didn't."

"No. The truth was, I didn't have a home to go back to. That was why I'd stowed away on that ship. To make a fresh start. New me, new life, new world." He laughed, his belly knotted with tension. "So, what do you think, *cara?* A sordid tale? A bad movie?"

"I think," Isabella said gently, "you must have been a brave, terrified, amazing boy." She reached for his hand. "You did what you had to do, and you made that new life for yourself."

A sweet sense of relief swept through him.

"I am happy you see that," he said softly.

"What happened after you stowed away? When you got to Brazil?"

"I made a plan."

"A plan?"

"I'd educate myself. Learn things that would help me find that new life. I began by studying Portuguese and English. I took some night classes. Math. Science. History. Business. I wasn't particular." He laughed. "I'd never tried putting anything in my head before so there was lots of room up there to fill. And I worked at every possible kind of job. Loading cargo. Construction. The oil fields. You name it, I did it. I took some risks, made a little bit of money, took some additional risk and made more. And I discovered I had a talent for—for organizing things."

"Like managing property."

His gut twisted.

"Something like that, yes."

"When did you meet Rio D'Aquila?"

When, indeed. Rio took a deep breath. He had to be careful now, very careful until tonight, when he could tell her everything.

"Remember the dot-com thing? The incredible rise in the stock market? Well, I'd played it. Invested in some of the companies. And—"

"And lost your money." Isabella sighed. "I remember."

The fact was, he hadn't lost anything. His investments had been wise ones; he'd made his first millions on that Wall Street stampede but if he told her that—

"Is that when you met D'Aquila?"

"Yes," he said, and damned if it wasn't true. He'd looked in the mirror, said goodbye to Matteo Rossi and hello to Rio D'Aquila, and he'd never looked back.

Until now.

"So, he offered you a job? Managing property for him?"

"It's probably more accurate to say I handle a variety of things for him."

"You like him."

"I, ah, I think we get along well enough."

"We. You say that so easily. Is he really a nice man?"

A good question. Rio felt a muscle knot in his jaw.

"I think he wants to be," he said, after a minute, "but there are lots of pressures on him."

"I guess he's not so awful. Here we are, using his plane."

Was a lie still a lie when it actually was the truth?

"Right," Rio said, "here we are, using his plane."

"But the villa we're going to… You said it's yours."

"Absolutely mine," he said without hesitation. "I bought it a long time ago with—with some winnings. It was the first home I'd ever owned." He reached for her hand and squeezed it. "It means a lot to me," he said gruffly. "But it will mean even more if you like it."

"I'll love it," Isabella said.

"Will you?" he said, his voice filled with relief.

How could she not? she thought, when she loved its owner with all her heart.

They reached Mustique in late afternoon.

Isabella's first glimpse of the island made her catch her breath.

Pale blue sky. Fluffy cotton clouds. A vivid blue sea, endless white beaches, lush emerald jungle. The colors of paradise, she thought happily.

An old Jeep was waiting for them at the small airport, keys dangling from the ignition. They got in and drove along a narrow road that climbed into the low hills. Just when it seemed as if the surrounding jungle was going to swallow them up, the trees opened onto a clearing and a graceful white building.

Matteo pulled the Jeep to a stop before it.

"Well," he said, as if his heart wasn't in his throat, "this is it."

"Oh," Isabella said, "oh, Matteo…"

He felt the tension within him ease, if only a little.

"You like it?"

"Like it?" She flung herself into his arms, gear-shift be damned. "It's wonderful! Like a painting. Something by, what's his name—"

"Gauguin?"

She laughed with delight. "Exactly."

"Si. Sim." He grinned. "Yes. I thought the same thing the first time I saw it. Want to get out and take—"

But Isabella was already out of the Jeep, her face alive with pleasure. Rio followed, and took her hand.

"Thank you," she said, her eyes shining, "for sharing this beautiful place with me."

She turned to him, lay a hand on his chest, rose on her toes and kissed him.

Rio felt his throat constrict.

Showing her the pool, the beach, the sea, could wait.

It was far more important to scoop her into his arms, carry her into the villa and make love to her with a tenderness that made her weep.

They fell asleep in each other's arms but when Isabella woke, she was alone.

Shadows had crept across the bedroom; she

could see the pink and violet of twilight through the open glass that led to the patio.

She could see her lover, as well.

Matteo stood at the teak railing, his back to her as he looked out over the sea.

The breeze ruffled his hair. He had thick, dark, short hair; she loved the feel of it under her hands.

She loved the feel of every part of him.

Her heart skipped a beat.

He was so strong, so masculine. He was a feast for her eyes and without him watching her, she could take all the time she wanted to enjoy the view.

Matteo wore faded jeans and a white T-shirt. The simple clothes emphasized his broad shoulders, long body, narrow hips and long, muscled legs.

He was—God, he was gorgeous.

And he was hers.

Not for forever. She knew that. They had not talked about forever; how could they, when they'd only just met? Still, the truth was that she was already his, forever, in her heart.

She thought of Anna, always cynical about men, and how she teased Isabella about her love life.

Her lack of a love life, to be accurate. Anna's teasing was a cover-up for sisterly concern.

You're waiting for Prince Charming, Iz, she'd say, *but there's a problem. He only exists in a fairy tale.*

Not true.

Pessimist or not, Anna had found her very own Prince Charming. Now, Isabella had found hers. Unfortunately, there was one huge difference. Anna and her prince had fallen in love. Isabella's story had not gone that way.

She'd fallen in love. Her prince had not.

Isabella sat up in the bed, sighed and thrust her hands into her hair, dragging the heavy mass back from her face.

Her prince was her lover but that wasn't the same as loving her. Okay. So be it. She was a grown-up, not a dreamy-eyed girl, and this wasn't a story, it was reality, and when it ended, she'd survive.

She'd survive. She'd have to survive, no matter how it hurt to think of a future without Matteo, and she must never let him know—

"Hey, sleepyhead. You're awake."

Quickly, she ran her hands over her eyes, turned toward him and forced a smile.

"Hi."

He sat down beside her, opened his arms and gathered her into his embrace.

"Mmm." He pressed his lips to her hair. "I love the way you smell when you wake up. All soft and female."

Her lips curved in a smile. "I like the way you smell, too. Sea and sky and Matteo." She leaned back in his arms and looked at him. "If only somebody could bottle that and turn it into cologne..."

He laughed. Then, his eyes searched hers.

"You really like it here, sweetheart?"

"How could I not? This beautiful island. This wonderful house." She smiled again. "And you. It's all perfect."

Rio linked his hands at the base of her spine.

"We can make it more perfect," he said softly.

"I don't see how."

"Dinner in a quiet little restaurant by the sea would be a start."

"Uh-huh. A quiet little restaurant, and me in those sweats." She laughed and wrinkled her nose.

"I think there might be Health Department rules to keep me out."

He grinned and planted a kiss on the end of her nose.

"I took care of that."

"You did, huh?"

"I did."

"You bribed the department of health?" she said, laughing.

"I bought you some stuff to wear."

"What?"

"I said, I bought you—"

"Matteo. You can't do that."

He smiled. "Too late. I already did."

"But—"

"A dress. One of those floaty things with skinny straps. Brown. Well, maybe it's amber. Or dark gold."

"Matteo, listen to me. You cannot—"

"Shorts. A couple of T-shirts. Sandals. I guessed at the sizes."

"Would you listen?"

"So I went with size sixteen for the clothes and size ten for the sandals."

"Matt—" Isabella slapped her hands against his

chest. "Size what for the clothes? And for the sandals? Do you really think—" Her eyes narrowed. "You're making that up."

"The part about the sizes?" He smiled. "Absolutely."

"But you really spent money on clothes for me? I can't let you do that. Really, I—"

"Really, you can. Things are inexpensive here." It was a lie of monumental proportions but what did one more matter? "I guessed at the sizes. And the colors." He nuzzled a curl from her cheek. "I ordered everything by phone, sweetheart, and they delivered it while you were sleeping. So if things don't fit, or if you don't like them—"

"If I don't like them? Are you crazy? I'm going to love them! How could you even think—"

Rio kissed her. Kissed her gently, then more deeply. She made a soft, sexy little sound; he groaned as she melted against him.

"Isabella," he whispered, and she fell back on the bed, her arms taking him down with her, and he made love to her as Matteo Rossi for the very last time because tonight, after he'd showed her off to the world...

Tonight, he was going to take the biggest risk of his life.

He was going to tell Isabella he'd been deceiving her.

And that he loved her, with all his heart.

A couple of thousand miles away, Anna Orsini Valenti was pacing the office at the rear of the bar her brothers owned in SoHo.

That she was able to pace it was proof of how carefully everyone else was maintaining their distance.

Eight of them—Anna, her husband, three of her brothers and their wives—were packed into the relatively small room.

The bar—*The Bar,* to use its semiofficial name—was still a real bar. Rafe, Dante, Falco and Nick had bought it for the express purpose of keeping it that way as the area all around it turned upscale and expensive.

They had done little to change it, and the little they had done had not included expanding the office. It was small. Very small. On a good day, all four brothers, big men every one, constituted a crowd.

"For the tenth time, Anna," Rafe said, "what's this all about?"

Anna glared at him.

"For the tenth time," she snapped, "I'll tell you once we're all here."

"Well, then," Falco said impatiently, "where in hell is Dante?"

"He's on his way, with Gabriella."

"And Izzy?"

"Izzy's not coming."

"Maybe Dante and Gaby aren't, either," Nick said logically. "Maybe they're away. Maybe they're out for the evening. Damnit, Anna—"

The office door edged open. Dante Orsini and his wife squeezed into the small room. One glance at Dante's grim face and Gaby's swollen eyes and the Orsini-Valenti clan fell silent.

"Okay," Rafe said grimly. "Let's hear it."

Anna took a deep breath. "Izzy phoned me this morning."

Nick: "So?"

"She phoned to tell me she was going away for the weekend."

Rafe: "And?"

"She was in Southampton."

Falco: "Southampton, Long Island? What was she doing all the way out there?"

Anna looked at Dante, who cleared his throat.

"She went to interview for a job. A landscaping job. We— I got her the interview."

"It was me," Gabriella Orsini said quickly, touching her husband's arm. "I thought it was a wonderful opportunity. It was such an important commission…"

"I'm the one, darling," Dante said softly. "It's entirely my fault, not yours."

"Goddamnit," Falco snarled. Elle, his beautiful wife, grabbed his hand and clutched it. "Will somebody get to the point?"

"I convinced Rio D'Aquila to add her to his short list of landscaping applicants."

"Rio D'Aquila?" Nick raised an eyebrow. "Smart guy. Lots of money. He's into shipping, freight, oil, computers—"

"He's into women, too," Rafe murmured. Chiara Orsini dug a sharp elbow into her husband's side. "Hey," he said, "I'm only saying what I've heard."

"You're right," Dante said tersely. "Lots of money. Lots of women. Not much heart."

"Well, so what?" Nick said. "The guy doesn't

have to pass a morals test before Iz can go to work for him."

Anna narrowed her eyes.

"Izzy drove out there yesterday. She took my car. She had some kind of accident."

A communal gasp almost sucked the air from the room.

"No," Anna said quickly, "she's fine. She's okay. But—"

"But?"

"She met someone. A man. And she called to tell me she was going away with him for the week."

Silence descended on the tiny room again.

Falco: "Wow."

Nick: "Our Izzy?"

Rafe: "Going away, with a guy?"

The brothers looked at each other.

"Well," Rafe said, "okay. I mean, she's a big girl. I mean, hell, we're happy for her. I mean—"

"His name," Anna said, "is Matteo Rossi."

Frowns all around. Nobody knew a Matteo Rossi.

"Who?" Nick's wife, Alessia, said.

"Exactly. So, I asked her, who was this Matteo

Rossi? And she said that Rossi worked for Rio D'Aquila. That he was the caretaker at D'Aquila's Southampton estate."

"A caretaker?" a male voice asked.

Throats were cleared.

"Okay," Falco said, "well, hell, we're not snobs—"

"Except," Dante said, "except, D'Aquila's caretaker is a guy named Bill Foster."

This time, the silence in the room was a palpable force.

"What the hell is going on?" Nick said softly. "Has Izzy been kidnapped?"

"Worse."

"Sweet Mary, what could be—"

"Matteo Rossi and Rio D'Aquila are the same man."

Rafe shook his head. "I don't understand."

"They're the same man, damnit! Anna called me, told me Iz had called and said that she was leaving the country with some stranger."

"Leaving the—"

"She didn't like how it sounded. Neither did I. So I tried to get hold of D'Aquila to see what he could tell me about Rossi."

"And?"

"And, I couldn't reach him. And something didn't smell right. And," Dante said, his voice becoming flat, "I decided to do some checking. I used that guy, the private investigator who's done some work for Orsini Brothers Investments in the past."

"And?" Falco said, through his teeth.

"D'Aquila's real name is Matteo Rossi. He's the man Izzy's gone away with. He lied to her, told her he's a caretaker, told her God only knows what other lies, and now she's in the middle of nowhere with him."

Silence wrapped around the office again. This time, it was ugly.

Isabella, sweetly innocent Isabella, the girl who worried over each flower she grew, who picked up half-dead plants left for the trash collector on the curb so she could nurse them back to life—she, the baby they all adored, had been seduced by a man reputed to be a heartless bastard, a man who had lied to her, who was pretending to be someone he wasn't—

"Why?" Draco said.

They were all bewildered. Was it a cruel joke? A

vicious prank? They talked. And postulated. And came up with only one obvious point of agreement.

Their Izzy needed them.

"They're not in the middle of nowhere," Anna said in a low voice. "They're on Mustique."

An hour later, the Orsinis' private jet was in the air.

CHAPTER ELEVEN

A LITTLE before eight, Isabella shooed her lover from the bedroom.

They had showered. Together, of course, which took a little longer—a lot longer—than if each had showered alone.

Matteo was shaved and dressed. Chino trousers. Dark brown moccasins with no socks. A black T-shirt that clung to his wide shoulders and hard body in a way that made her want to drag him down into the rumpled sheets, but he'd made dinner reservations at what he said was "just a restaurant" and said it in a way that made her suspect it was much more than that.

She knew he was spending far too much money and she'd tried to come up with a way to split costs. But she came from a family of strong, proud and, yes, occasionally arrogant brothers. Matteo had those same qualities and she'd decided it was best to let him spoil her, at least for a little while.

Besides, the selfish truth was that it felt lovely to be spoiled by a man like him.

So she let him bend her back over his arm for a dramatic kiss that made her laugh, and then she banished him to the patio.

"Give me fifteen minutes."

Her gorgeous, sexy, amazing lover rolled his eyes. "A likely story."

She grinned, he grinned back, stole one last quick kiss and went out the glass doors to the patio.

Isabella shut the doors. She wanted to look perfect for him, and to make her entrance a surprise.

How many other women had made him wait while they dressed? A legion, she thought as she dropped the bath towel she'd wrapped around her on the bed.

Matteo probably had to beat the women off with a stick—or with a kind word, because she couldn't imagine him not being less than honorable in his dealings with anyone.

She had only to think of how honorable, how honest he'd been with her, telling her things about himself most men would try to keep buried. On top of that, he was gorgeous. Generous. Kind. Sexy as a man could be.

He was a modern Prince Charming—and he was hers. For tonight, for the next few days…

Don't think too far ahead, Isabella.

No. She wouldn't. But there was always a chance. What good were fairy tales, if one didn't occasionally come true?

The clothes he'd bought her were laid out on a love seat in the corner of the bedroom.

They were beautiful. And he'd thought of everything. Well, almost. No comb and brush, but she had used his. No makeup but she rarely wore makeup anyway. Besides, lovemaking had left her eyes and skin glowing, and her lover's kisses had left her lips rosy pink and delicately swollen.

The rest? Well, yes, he'd remembered to get panties.

But no bra.

Her heart did a little stutter step.

She'd just have to wear this bit of silk, this dress that reminded her of gossamer-winged lavender and blue butterflies, without one.

Her breasts would be bare behind the thin fabric. When Matteo spoke to her in a low, husky voice, when he took her in his arms, he'd be able to see the effect he had on her.

Isabella let out a shaky breath.

Amazing. She was turning herself on just by thinking about him, and who'd ever imagined that?

The dress fit as if it had been made for her. So did the sandals of soft gold leather with delightfully wicked heels. She fluffed her hair, sent up a silent thank-you to whichever of the Fates it was who'd decreed that her long, dark curls would not, for once in her life, turn to frizz.

There could not be a woman on the entire planet even half as happy as she was tonight.

Fifteen minutes, Isabella had said.

Rio knew what a woman's fifteen minutes meant, that the actual time could run to an hour or more. But a quarter hour later, he heard the doors slide open. He turned around—

And there she was.

My God, he thought, in English and Portuguese and Italian and half a dozen other languages he'd picked up doing business around the world, *My God, how beautiful she is!*

Her hair, black and lustrous, fell in sexy curls over her shoulders. Her eyes were wide, glittering as if they were filled with starlight. And the dress...

Dio, the dress.

Over the years, he had spent thousands on couturier designs for his mistresses. This dress had cost him an almost pitiful fraction of that, but he was certain that *Vogue* or any fashion magazine would have fought for the privilege of taking a photo of it now.

Except, he thought, as he drank in the sight, except it wasn't the dress that was special. It was his gorgeous, sweet, sexy Isabella.

Her smile turned questioning.

"What do you think?" she said. "Do I look—"

Rio swept her into his arms, angled his mouth over hers and kissed her. She made one of those little sounds that drove him half-crazy; her arms went around his neck and she returned his kiss with such passion, such honesty that he could have sworn he felt the earth tilt.

He kissed her again but it wasn't enough. Not even taking her to bed again would have been enough because—

Because he loved her.

He had known it on the plane. Now, the realization swam in his blood.

He loved her.

Deeply. With everything he was, everything he had ever been or would ever be. He loved her, and it was time he told her the truth.

"Sweetheart," he said softly, "Isabella *mia*…"

"I want to look beautiful for you tonight," she whispered.

"You are more than beautiful, sweetheart."

"You think?"

He smiled. "I know."

And he knew, too, that all the things he had to tell her could wait. She deserved this night, a perfect night. Lovers going out for dinner, sharing a bottle of wine, holding each other close on a tiny dance floor.

Then he'd bring her home, and embark on a voyage that would make that long-ago trip in the forecastle of a rusting freighter seem simple.

He would bare his soul and his heart to the woman he adored, and pray she'd forgive him for his lies.

* * *

Isabella was almost dizzy with joy.

An ivory moon had risen majestically from a turquoise sea after the sun had made a spectacular exit over the horizon. The air was warm and scented with flowers.

Matteo drove them to a tiny restaurant that seemed to hang over a sea that rolled in on a whisper of sound that spoke of ancient mysteries.

The night and the setting were wonderful but *wonderful* was not sufficient to describe the man who was her lover.

He was all a woman could dream of or want.

Not just the way he looked, though she had to admit to a moment of foolish pride when they'd been shown to their table in this casual but elegant little place and all the women in it had given him looks of longing.

I agree, Isabella thought, *he's spectacular—and he's all mine.*

Maybe it made more sense to say, she was all his.

And oh, if only he wanted to be hers…

Thinking like that was dangerous. She knew that it was. They were in a sexual relationship and she wasn't naive, she understood that, too. But—

But maybe, just maybe, Matteo felt more for her than desire. He had to, otherwise how could he make her feel as if she were the center of his universe?

When the captain took them to their table and started to pull out her chair, Matteo politely demurred, moved forward and pulled it out himself.

His hands brushed over her shoulders; he moved her chair in and, as he did, he stroked his thumb lightly over the hollow in her throat.

Her breath caught.

His touch sent a rush of desire through her body. He knew it; she felt her nipples peak and his gaze dropped to her breasts and when he looked up at her again, his eyes burned with flame.

"I'm going to have a lot of trouble keeping my hands off you tonight," he said in a rough whisper.

Just that—his words, his glance—and Isabella felt herself go hot and wet.

"Good," she whispered back, and the flames in his eyes narrowed to pinpoints of light.

He ordered for them both.

"Is that all right, *cara?*"

She, the woman who bristled when one of her own brothers was foolish enough to think he could decide if she wanted a burger or a hot dog at a Fourth of July barbecue, she smiled and said that would be fine.

His choices were eclectic and wonderful. A drink that tasted deliciously of coconut and rum arrived in a tall glass garnished with gorgeous flowers. A cold fruit soup dotted with freshly ground black pepper, a combination that seemed incongruous until she tasted it, was next. And then white wine that was cool and crisp, crab cakes hot with spices, pan-blackened grouper, bananas sautéed in butter and cinnamon and nutmeg and who knew what else.

The meal was decadently delicious.

The service was wonderful.

But being with Matteo…

No words could do that justice.

They ate. They talked. They laughed. And, in between, Matteo led her onto a miniscule dance floor where he wrapped his arms around her, gathered her close against him, and they swayed in rhythm to soft music.

Isabella sighed as he drew her to him, as she felt his hard body against the softness of hers, his muscled thighs against the length of hers.

She put her arms around his neck. He put one hand in her hair, the other at the base of her spine.

She buried her face against him, inhaling him, feeling him harden against her, feeling the power of knowing she could make him want her just by being in his arms.

It happened over and over. Dancing, or pretending to dance. The teasing of him against her, her against him, until they were both half out of their minds.

Isabella moaned.

"Matteo," she whispered, "take me to bed."

Rio had done a lot of tough things in his life but nothing compared to getting off that dance floor without lifting her in his arms, taking her down to the beach and making love to her right there.

Somehow, he managed to hang on to what little sanity he had left. He clasped her hand, never broke stride as he dug a handful of bills from his pocket and dropped them on the table.

He drove home fast, his hand under her skirt, her hand on him, taking the narrow, curving roads at speeds his brain warned were dangerous, even when he wasn't almost blind with desire, but all that mattered was getting home.

When they reached the villa, he drew her from the car before she had time to get her door open.

"Isabella," he said, just that, because her name was infused with everything a man could need or want.

She went into his arms.

He held her to him, kissed her mouth and throat. And fought to hang on to his control.

"Isabella." He drew back, framed her face with his hands. "Sweetheart, we have to talk."

"Not now," she said in a broken whisper, and when she went up on her toes, dug her hands into his hair and kissed him, her mouth open and hot and greedy against his, Rio forget everything except his need for her.

There would be plenty of time, later.

He carried her through the dark house to the bedroom where they tore at each other's clothes.

When they were naked, she moved against him.

"Now," she said, and the urgency in her voice all but finished him.

They fell to the bed in each other's arms and made love, again and again and again, while the moon sailed across the heavens and the earth spun through the mantle of the night…

And, fell asleep, at last, wrapped in each other's arms.

Isabella came awake abruptly from a deep, dreamless sleep. The moon had set. The night had turned black and impenetrable.

Something had awakened her—

A sound. A noise. Something growling just beneath the hiss of the waves rolling in from the sea.

She recognized it now. What she heard was a car, coming up the narrow road to the villa—and where was Matteo? She was alone in the big bed.

Fear turned her skin icy.

She sat up quickly, grabbed the first thing at hand—a cotton throw from the foot of the bed—and wrapped it around herself.

"Matteo?" she whispered as she padded out of the bedroom. "Matteo? Where—"

A hand closed around her wrist.

"Easy, sweetheart. I'm right here."

Her heart felt as if it were going to burst from her chest. Her lover had all but materialized from the shadows in the hallway; her eyes had adjusted to the dark and she saw that he'd pulled on a pair of jeans and nothing else.

Shivering, Isabella moved closer to him.

"It's a car, isn't it? Who—"

"I don't know," Rio said, and, damnit, he didn't.

Who would come to the villa in the middle of the night? Crime was practically nonexistent on the island but things happened, no matter how safe and tucked away a place seemed.

"Matteo. I'm frightened."

He was, too. Not for himself. For her. A dozen ugly headlines, splashed across newspapers everywhere, shot through his mind.

"Don't be," he said. "It's probably nothing. Kids out, having fun. Or somebody tipsy who made the wrong turn." He put his hand against her cheek. "Isabella. I want you to go into the bedroom and lock the—"

"No! I'm not leaving you."

The sound of the engine died and the night filled with silence. A car door slammed, and then another.

"Isabella," Rio said urgently, "get inside that room and lock yourself in."

"I am not leaving you, Matteo. Whatever happens, I want to be with you."

Rio's heart swelled with love.

"Ah, Izzy," he said softly, "Izzy, sweetheart—"

A fist hammered against the door. "Open up!"

A heavy wooden statue stood on a table near the door. It wasn't a hell of a good weapon, but it was all there was. Rio grabbed it.

"Isabella," he hissed, "go into the bedroom and—"

Bam! "You open this effing door or—" *Bam!* "—you effing son of a bitch, or so help me God—" *Bam!* "—I'll break it down!"

Isabella stiffened. No. It couldn't be—

"D'Aquila, you no good, sleazy, bastard! I've come for my sister. If I have to take this place apart to get to her, I will!"

Isabella stared at her lover.

"That's—that's my brother," she said. "But what's he doing here?"

"D'Aquila!"

The door shuddered under Dante Orsini's fist.

"He thinks—" She shook her head. "He thinks you're Rio D'Aquila."

"Isabella," Rio said in a low voice, "Isabella, you must listen to me."

"My God, what a mess!" Isabella gave an unsteady laugh. "My brother, come to rescue his little sister from the clutches of big, bad Rio D'Aquila... I'm so sorry, Matteo!" She moved past him, reached for the lock on the door. "I'm horrified. Humiliated. I don't know how this could have happ—"

"Isabella!" Rio caught her by the shoulder. She could feel each finger digging into her flesh. "Don't open that door."

"What do you mean, don't open it? I know this is awful but he's got things all wrong. I most certainly don't need rescuing. He had no right to come here. And you most certainly are not—"

"But I am," Rio said. "I am Rio D'Aquila."

Isabella stared at him. He saw the color drain from her face. Her lips formed a word—*No*—but it was soundless.

Rio cursed violently. He dropped the wooden statue and reached for her but she stumbled back. *Cristo,* he was running out of time! The pounding at the door had stopped, but he wasn't foolish enough to think Dante Orsini had gone away.

He knew he had only minutes to explain everything. How what had started as a farce had become all that mattered, all that ever would matter for the rest of his life.

"It's true," he said in a low voice. "I am Rio."

Isabella shook her head. Her eyes were wide with disbelief.

"No. You're not. You're not! You're his caretaker. His property manager. His pilot. You're Matteo Rossi."

"*Si. Sim.* I am him, as well. Matteo Rossi is my real name. Hell, not my real name. It's the name I was given. I took the name Rio D'Aquila years ago." Desperate, he ran his hands through his hair. "Isabella *mia*. Sweetheart, it's all so damned complicated—"

Tears ran down her face.

"Why?" she whispered. Her voice broke. "Why did you lie to me? Why did you let me think—"

Glass shattered in the bedroom. Rio knew it meant that Dante Orsini had broken open the patio doors, that he had only seconds left.

"Why?" she said. Her voice rose to a sobbing cry. "Why?"

"I don't know. It was on the spur of the moment. It was nothing—"

"Nothing?"

"Yes. No. It was—it was a harmless prank."

"A prank," she said, through bloodless lips.

"We were strangers. We were never going to see each other again. And then—and then—"

Dante stormed toward Rio, eyes blazing.

"You SOB," he snarled, and hit Rio with a fist that felt as if it were made of iron.

Rio staggered back but his eyes never left Isabella's.

"I wanted to tell you. I tried to tell you. Even tonight—"

"A prank," she whispered, while her heart shattered. "Pretending to be someone you weren't. Telling me we were in his house when it was yours. Telling me stories about how you'd come to be working for him—"

"Isabella, please, I beg you—"

"And—and you—you made love to me…"

A sob broke from her throat. Rio groaned and reached for her; Dante put a hand in the center of his chest and pushed him back.

"Iz," Dante said harshly, "Anna's outside. Get out of this house, go to her and wait in the car."

"No," Rio shouted. "Don't listen to him. Stay where you are. Let me talk to you. Let me explain—"

"You already did," Isabella whispered. "You said it was nothing. You said it was a prank."

"I wanted to tell you. A dozen times. A hundred. But—"

"When?" Isabella said brokenly. "Before you seduced me? Or after?"

Dante hit him again. It was a good, solid shot. Rio, who was a boxer, could have put Dante down with one blow. Instead, he snarled with pain, anger and rage.

At himself.

"I made a terrible mistake, *cara*. What I did was wrong. And not admitting to it sooner was cowardly but—"

Isabella had stopped listening. He could see it happen, that she was gathering herself together, leaving him behind. She had never looked more beautiful than now, standing straight and proud, her chin lifted, wearing the cotton throw as if it were a queen's cloak.

"Orsini," Rio said desperately, "give us five minutes alone."

"Not in this lifetime," Dante growled. "Iz? We're leaving, baby. You just take my arm and—"

"Amazing," Isabella said. "Here I thought I was the one playing games."

Rio blinked. "What?"

"A caretaker. A man who lives in another man's home, eats another man's food, takes another man's orders."

"No. I'm telling you, I am—"

"Oh, I believe you. You're Rio D'Aquila."

Isabella's voice had turned chill and smooth. She smiled, and told herself that all she had to do was get through the next couple of minutes and then this would all be nothing more than a bad dream.

"And I—I enjoyed our little idyll but the thing is, if I'd know who you really were, I'd probably never have bothered with you in the first place."

She saw the man she knew as Matteo narrow his eyes. Good. Better than good. But it wasn't enough. She wanted to put the knife in deep and then give it a twist.

"I mean, men with lots of money, you know, power brokers like Rio D'Aquila, are a dime a dozen in my world." She forced a smile; she hoped it held amusement and not anguish. "But guys with dirt under their nails, studs like Matteo Rossi—"

"Izzy," her brother said softly, "honey, it's okay. Just go outside to Anna."

"Dante can tell you," she said, putting her hand on her brother's rigid-with-fury arm, praying he wouldn't spoil the lie. "I'm not exactly the little innocent you decided I was."

"Iz." Her brother's voice was rough. "Iz, honey—"

"I wanted something different. Well, Matteo Rossi was different. And—and it was fun," Isabella said, and prayed her voice would not break into the same tiny shards as her heart. "But you used me. You lied to me. And I'll despise you for it, for the rest of my life."

Rio's face had gone blank. Isabella looked at her brother.

"Dante," she said, "leave him alone. He's not worth the effort."

Somehow, she made it to the door. She heard Dante say something sharp and ugly. Then they were outside, where the air was cool and clean and she could let the darkness enfold her.

"Izzy," someone said, "oh, Izzy, baby…"

"Anna," Isabella whispered.

Anna's arms opened wide. She flew into them and then, only then, was it safe to give way to racking sobs.

CHAPTER TWELVE

ISABELLA knelt in the middle of her sister's penthouse garden, carefully pulling weeds and deadheading spent flower blossoms.

She was dripping with sweat, her back ached, the light-headedness and vague nausea that had plagued her for the past couple of weeks seemed ever-present, but she'd be damned if she'd give in to a summer virus when she had so much work to do.

Summer could be tough in New York.

Pavement. Concrete. Skyscrapers that created man-made canyons trapped the heat and reflected it back with the ferocity of a gigantic convection oven.

The result was predictable.

Horns blared, tempers rose, pedestrians wilted.

So did plants. Isabella always warned her clients about that.

"Plants are living things," she'd say. "They need

food some of the time and unless they're succulents, they need water all of the time, especially in summer."

She gave them handsome calendars filled with instructions on caring for their gardens if they didn't hire her to do it for them and when summer arrived, she emailed cheerful reminders to water, water, water.

Some people, she thought grumpily, didn't get the message.

An end-of-season heat wave had the city in its cruel clutches. Isabella's phone rang and rang with desperate pleas for help.

My hydrangeas are dying!

You know that green and yellow shrub with the funny leaves? Well, the leaves are all brown and now they're falling off!

And there was always her favorite complaint: *Really, Ms. Orsini, we are very upset! You said these flowers would last forever!*

Nothing lasts forever, Isabella had finally told a caller after one angry voice mail too many.

Because, of course, nothing did.

"Hell," she muttered, and sat back on her heels. She was not going there.

Ridiculous, that after four weeks she could still say something, see something, hear something and just like that, the entire horrible interlude with Rio D'Aquila would pop into her mind.

The Horrible Interlude.

Isabella snorted, ran the back of her hand over her dripping forehead, then gave another dig to a particularly hardy weed.

It sounded like a bad movie title but what else would you call what had happened? *Interludis Horribilis?*

She laughed.

Not bad, she thought, not at all bad—and then her throat tightened and what had started as laughter turned into a lump and she heard herself make a pathetic little sound, really pathetic, painfully pathetic—

"Izzy, for God's sake, what are you doing out here?"

Isabella shaded her eyes with a grimy hand and looked up. Anna stood over her, looking cool and elegant in a silk suit and high heeled pumps.

"Anna," she said brightly. "You're home."

"It's after six. Even lawyers know when to knock off for the day. What are you doing?"

"Playing in the dirt. Or trying to save your pansies. Which does it look like?"

"What it looks like," Anna said, "is that you're trying to get sunstroke. For goodness sake, come inside. Those pansies are fine. You said so yourself last week."

"Exactly. Haven't you touched them at all since then? Thinned them out? Weeded them? Watered them?"

"Draco did."

"Nobody did. Honestly, Anna—"

"Honestly, Izzy, enough is enough. Get up and come inside."

"Ask me nicely and I might."

"What?"

"I'm not a child, Anna. I know you mean well, but—" Isabella sighed. "Never mind. Just give me another couple of minutes."

"You're very prickly lately, Iz."

"I'm not prickly at all," Isabella snapped. Anna rolled her eyes and Isabella let out a long breath. "Look, I don't want your flowers to die, okay?"

"So you had to pick the hottest day of the year to give them a manicure?"

"It's not a manicure. And this was the first

chance I had to come by. I've been so busy with other idiots that—"

"Other idiots?" Anna folded her arms. "That's really nice."

"Hell," Isabella said wearily. "Okay. Point made. It's time to call it a day."

"Good. Come sit inside and we'll have some iced— Izzy?" Anna grabbed Isabella's arm as her sister swayed like a sapling in a breeze. "My God, you're white as a sheet."

"I'm—I'm okay. I got up too fast. The sun. And being on my knees all this time—"

Anna put her arm around Isabella and led her into the cool comfort of the penthouse living room.

"Sit down on that chair. I'll get some water."

"I'm filthy," Isabella said shakily.

"Sit down," Anna said in her best courtroom voice.

Isabella sat.

The room was spinning and her stomach was somewhere just slightly south of her throat. She bent forward, shut her eyes and took long, deep breaths.

Okay. She'd have to deal with this summer virus.

Because it *was* a summer virus. It had to be.

"Here you go."

Anna pressed a tall glass of iced water into Isabella's hands. She drank it slowly. Over the past few days she'd learned, the hard way, that when she felt like this, even a drink of water might trigger a gag reaction.

"Better?"

Isabella nodded. "Yes, thank you. Much better."

"It's a good thing I came along when I did. You'd still be out there, working in the Sahara and saving our pansies." Anna peered at her younger sister. "You look like hell."

"Thank you."

"Okay, here's what we're going to do," Anna said briskly, taking the glass from Isabella. "You take a nice cool shower, I'll give you something to wear and then we'll have a glass of Pinot Grigio while we wait for Draco to come home. We're having broiled halibut for supper and—Izzy?"

Isabella ran for the powder room and made it just in time to slam the door and bend over the toilet before her stomach emptied itself of the crackers and chicken soup she'd managed to get down for lunch.

She flushed the bowl. Washed out her mouth, washed her hands and face. Her reflection was not reassuring. Her cheeks were colorless, her hair was wild—and the worst was yet to come.

She had to face Anna.

A long, deep breath. Then she opened the bathroom door. Her sister was standing right outside, arms folded, expression grim, looking exactly the way Isabella felt—

As if the world as they both knew it was about to end.

"You're pregnant," Anna said flatly.

Isabella tried for a laugh. "You certainly have a way with words."

"You," Anna repeated, "are pregnant."

"I just said—"

"I heard what you said, and it wasn't 'no, I'm not.' Answer me, Izzy. Did that lying SOB get you pregnant?"

Isabella narrowed her eyes. "He didn't 'get' me anything! I'm a grown woman. I'm responsible for myself."

"Damnit, answer the question! Are you pregnant?"

"This is not a courtroom, and I am not on the witness stand!"

"Meaning?"

"Meaning…" Isabella's shoulders slumped. "Meaning, I don't know."

"What do you mean, you don't know?"

"Read my lips. I mean, I—don't—know."

"How can you not know? Have you missed your period? Have you seen a doctor? Bought an EPT? It is not possible to answer a question like, 'Are you pregnant?' by saying, 'I don't know.'"

"It is, if you're a coward."

"Oh, Iz…"

"See? This is why I didn't want to tell you. That 'oh, Iz,' as if you were thirteen and I were twelve and I'd just spilled your favorite nail polish all over your favorite sweater."

"Izzy, honey—"

"And that. That look. That tone. 'Izzy, honey,' meaning 'Izzy, you pathetic little incompetent, you sad underachiever, what have you done now?'"

Anna threw up her hands in defense. "I never—"

"Maybe not, but that's how it always sounds."

"How *what* always sounds? Izzy—"

"And that's another thing. My name is Isabella."

The sisters stared at each other.

"We need to talk," Anna finally said.

Isabella nodded and Anna led the way to the kitchen. Isabella sat at the glass-topped table. Anna poured another glass of iced water and gave it to her, started to pour water for herself, muttered "to hell with it" and instead took an opened bottle of Pinot Grigio from the fridge and poured herself half a tumbler of it.

Then she plopped into a chair opposite Isabella's.

"I have never," she said softly, "not once in our entire lives, thought you were anything less than smart, capable and altogether competent. Okay? I mean, let's get that out of the way first."

Isabella used her damp glass to make a ring of intersecting circles on the tabletop.

"You're my sister," Anna continued. "My baby sister, and—"

"I'm your sister," Isabella said, looking up. "And you're mine. And I love you like crazy, but—"

"But," Anna said, "you're all grown up. And I need to remember that."

"You do." Isabella gave a little laugh. "Except

when my stuff isn't as grown up as I am, and I need to borrow your clothes or your car…"

Her smile faded. Anna reached for her hand.

"Which takes us," she said gently, "back to the beginning."

Isabella nodded. "The old square one."

"You want to tell me about it?"

Isabella hesitated. Then she swallowed hard.

"More than anything," she said, and the entire sad story tumbled out. It took a while, because she had not told anyone anything after Dante and Anna had brought her back to the States.

But she knew the time had come.

She told Anna how she'd gotten stuck in traffic en route to Southampton. How she'd gotten lost. The accident that had left her on foot. How she'd stumbled through the gate at Rio D'Aquila's estate hours late.

"And D'Aquila was waiting for you," Anna said grimly.

"I didn't know who he was," Isabella said. "He was just a guy." *A big, shirtless, gorgeous sexy-looking guy…*

"Go on."

Isabella cleared her throat.

"We talked. And talked. He was—"

"Rude. Insolent."

"Actually, he was charming. He was fun. And then—"

"And then, he seduced you."

He kissed me, Isabella thought, *God, he kissed me and I melted...*

"No. He didn't. I—I left. And he came after me. It was dark by then and he said—he said he'd take me to the train station."

"But he didn't, the no-good, testosterone-crazed SOB."

"He did. Trouble was, the trains weren't running."

Anna snorted. "How could you have bought such a lie?"

"It was true. The station was closed. So, he said I could spend the night—"

"And then he seduced you."

"He showed me to a guest room and he gave me something to wear. I was a mess, your suit all torn and dirty—and I'm sorry about that. I'll pay you back—"

"Forget the suit," Anna snapped. "I'll just bet he gave you something to wear, something left over from some other damsel in distress who'd spent the night in his—"

"He gave me one of his sweat suits. And then we went to the kitchen—"

"Naturally. Men like him always want a woman manacled to the stove with a skillet in her free hand."

"Anna," Isabella said carefully, "you think you're being just a little judgmental here? Actually, *he* did the cooking. But we never got around to eating much because—"

"Because he sed—"

"My God," Isabella said, yanking her hand free of her sister's, "will you let me talk? Because we quarreled. But you're right. We did get around to seduction…" Isabella's voice trembled. "And I'm not really sure who seduced who."

Anna stared at her sister. "Please," she said, "please, *please* do not tell me you think you still feel something for this man!"

"Of course not."

"Because he has the morals of the manure you use for fertilizer."

"I don't feel anything for him, but he's not— not…"

"Izzy. I mean, Isabella, how can you say that? He seduced you, and don't waste your breath saying you were equally responsible. You don't know a thing about sex, Iz. And he—"

"He knew everything," Isabella whispered. "And it was—it was wonderful."

Anna Orsini Valenti looked at her sister. *Ohmygod,* she thought, and grabbed her hand again.

"Isabella," Anna said firmly. "You're forgetting all the rest. He spirited you out of the States."

Isabella laughed.

"Okay, so that sounds dumb. What I mean is, he took you away from everything familiar, everything that could have kept you safe—"

"He kept me safe. I'd never felt that safe in my life. When I was with him, when he held me in his arms… Can you possibly understand what I mean?"

Anna could. She had only to think of how it felt each time her husband touched her, and she understood.

In fact, she was starting to think she understood everything.

Her sister—her baby sister, though she wouldn't

make the mistake of calling her that ever again, had fallen head over heels for a rat.

"Yes," she said gently, "I do understand. But you're leaving something out, honey. He lied to you. And it was one hell of a lie, pretending he was someone he wasn't."

Isabella shook her head. "He didn't."

"He did! He's Rio D'Aquila but he told you he was Matteo Rossi."

"He's both. Matteo Rossi was the name the orphanage gave him." Isabella's eyes glittered with sorrow. "Can you imagine being raised in an orphanage?"

Anna could come close. Her own husband had been raised in a boarding school that seemed, each time she thought about it, straight out of a Dickens novel.

"He never lied, Anna. Not about what mattered, not after we'd become lovers. He told me the villa was his, and it was. He told me about his life as Matteo Rossi, and what he told me was the truth. And—and he would have told me the rest, if we'd had time."

"You had plenty of time. Three days—"

"Two days. And two nights. And that last night,

he kept saying we had to talk, that it was important, but I wouldn't listen. I just wanted to—to be
in his arms, to be with him because I—because I
loved him, God, I loved him—"

Isabella began to weep. Anna came around the
table, knelt beside her and took her in her arms.

"Oh, honey," she said softly.

"I still love him," Isabella said. "I always will.
And sometimes—sometimes I think he was starting to fall in love with me. Oh, God, Anna, if I'd
let him talk to me. If I'd said 'yes' when he asked
Dante to give us time alone." Her voice broke. "If
I hadn't lied to him because I'll never forget how
he looked when I said those terrible things…"

"What terrible things?"

"I was so hurt. I was in agony." Isabella drew a
shuddering breath. "So I lied. I said I'd never have
bothered with him if I knew who he was. I made
it clear that I'd been slumming by—by sleeping
with a man I thought was—was socially beneath
me."

"Oh, Iz!"

"And I said—I said I'd let him think I was—I
was sexually naive but that I wasn't."

"Oh, Iz!"

"I hurt him. I could see it. His feelings, his pride, the whole male thing. You know that whole male thing?"

Anna thought of her husband, the man she'd thought of as the Ice Prince. She thought of her brothers, the strength of their characters—and the fragility of their male egos.

"Oh, Iz!"

Isabella drew back and looked at Anna.

"I told you not to call me that," she said on a sad little laugh, and Anna burst into tears and wept with her.

That was how Draco found them a little while later.

"What happened?" he asked in bewilderment, and his beautiful wife said he would never under- stand, and then she relented and said okay, they'd tell him. And they did—well, not everything, not about the possibility of Isabella being preg- nant.

But they told him all the rest, that Isabella hated Rio D'Aquila except she didn't hate him, and they were right. He didn't understand.

All he understood was that men were helpless at moments like this, which was when he went to the phone and called his brother-in-law, Dante Orsini.

CHAPTER THIRTEEN

THE four Orsini brothers were sitting in their favorite booth at The Bar, their place in SoHo. Their brother-in-law, Prince Draco Valenti, was with them.

The booths at The Bar were big, easily accommodating six adults, but the men of the Orsini clan were all tall, broad-shouldered and long-legged. The result was that they were crammed into what should have been a sufficient space but wasn't.

It would have been nice to think that was why they were all glowering at each other, but they knew better.

They had a problem to deal with, and not one of them wanted to touch it.

So they ordered hamburgers and beer, but the burgers remained untouched.

The beer, on the other hand, was getting a good workout.

And the silence was almost deafening.

Raffaele and Falco seated at the ends of the booth, finally got to their feet, took away the hamburgers, the empty beer mugs and bottles, and came back with fresh liquid supplies.

Dante took that as a signal.

"Okay," he said, as his brothers slid back into the booth. "Let's get this over with."

Nicolo nodded. "Damned right. Not that it's gonna take very long. What I think is that Izzy's kind of dealing with post traumatic shock. She just needs time, is all."

"I agree," Rafe said. "Hell, when you think of what she went through—"

"Think all you like," Dante said. "The bottom line is that Anna suspects we may have overreacted."

There were snorts of disbelief all around the big, scarred wooden table.

"We sure as hell underreacted," Falco said coldly. "We should have all flown to Mustique with you and beaten the crap out of D'Aquila." His dark eyes narrowed. "It's still not too late for that."

There were murmurs of agreement, but Nick held up his hand.

"We agreed to leave him alone, remember? For Izzy's sake. She said she just wanted to forget he existed."

"Well, what's changed?"

Dante shrugged.

"Anna and Izzy had a talk. Draco came in on the tail end of it."

Draco nodded.

"And? What did Izzy tell you?"

Draco laughed, though it was not a happy sound.

"You ever try and get a woman who doesn't want to tell you something to tell it to you?"

Sighs all around the table.

"Okay," Rafe said. "Then, how did Iz seem to you? Like she was still carrying the torch for this guy?"

Draco looked at his brothers-in-law. He had been accepted as one of them and he knew it was an honor. They were smart, tough, successful men who adored their wives as much as he adored his.

Until last night, he'd felt as they did, that the man who'd broken Isabella's heart should have been drawn and quartered.

But what he'd seen in his sister-in-law's face the

prior evening had been raw emotion, and what his wife had told him afterward had given him pause.

There'd been a time he, too, had believed the woman he loved despised him, a time he'd come to this very place with his heart on display, knowing that he had to make the Orsini brothers understand that he loved his Anna, that nothing would keep him from loving her, no matter what they did to him.

"Draco? What do you think?"

Draco cleared his throat.

"I think Isabella is deeply in love with Rio D'Aquila or Matteo Rossi or whatever you want to call him," he said quietly.

"I know what to call him," Falco said. "He's nothing but a scheming, lying—"

"What you mean is," Rafe said, "is that she's infatuated with him. Okay. I guess that's understandable. She's just a baby and—"

"She's a grown woman," Draco said. "She made that point to Anna." He grinned. "With enough fervor that Anna was still apologizing for treating her as if she wasn't when they shooed me out of the room."

"Anna, apologizing?" Dante grinned, too. "I'd have paid to see that."

"Yeah," Falco said, "well, even if Iz thinks she loves the bastard, he's still a bastard."

"You really have a way with words," Nick said drily.

"Come on, dude, you know what I mean. Besides, D'Aquila or Rossi or whoever he is, doesn't give a damn for our Izzy."

"And you know this because…?" Rafe said.

"Well," Falco said, "where is he? A man who cares about a woman doesn't just let her go."

Falco's brothers looked at him.

"Okay," he said, the color rising in his face, "but it was different with Elle and me."

"Uh-huh."

"It was. Besides, we're talking about a whole other situation. The fact is, the bastard hasn't made any attempt to contact Iz, and—"

"You're right, he hasn't," a husky, slightly accented male voice said. "He's been much too busy nursing his wounded pride."

Startled, Rafe, Dante, Nick, Falco and Draco turned toward the man who'd appeared beside their booth. He was tall, same as them. Powerfully built, same as them. Dark-haired, same as them. He wore a custom-tailored suit, same as them.

And, in a heartbeat, they knew who he was.

Falco shot to his feet.

"D'Aquila," he snarled.

Rio nodded. "Yes."

The others rose, jostling each other as they got to their feet in the crowded booth.

"What the hell are you doing here?" Dante said coldly.

"I'm here to talk to you. All of you."

Cristo, Rio could almost smell the adrenaline in the air. Every muscle in his body was on alert.

"Back there," Nick growled, jerking his head toward the rear of The Bar.

The men surrounded Rio and led him to a door. *Dead man walking,* he thought, and knew that could end up pretty close to the truth.

If Isabella's brothers, plus the one additional guy he vaguely recognized as some sort of financial guru with a title, wanted to beat the crap out of him and leave him in the alley he figured was beyond that door, so be it.

He deserved it.

But the door opened into a small, very plain

office. A hand shoved him forward, the door slammed behind him, and then the five men faced him, faces like stone, arms folded, legs planted slightly apart.

Rio stood with his hands at his sides.

"So, this is the SOB, Rio D'Aquila," one of the men growled.

"Maybe he prefers his alias," another man snarled.

"Not that it matters," a third added.

"It damned well doesn't," a fourth said, "because he's going to be hurting really bad, whatever he calls himself."

Rio nodded. "Fists first, facts later? That's fine, if that's what you want, but at least leave me conscious long enough so I can tell you why I'm here."

Nobody laughed but then, Rio hadn't meant it as a joke.

It had taken him three weeks to get past his rage at being used by Isabella, another week before he'd let himself feel the pain of what had happened—

And then, finally, a couple of days ago, he'd come to his senses.

He didn't believe a word she'd said about sleeping with him because he was socially beneath her. That absolutely was not his Isabella.

As for her having pretended to be inexperienced—he didn't believe that, either. And even if she had been sexually experienced, it wouldn't have mattered.

He loved her. He adored her.

And she loved him.

What else could possibly matter?

Her love for him had been in her smile, her touch, her voice, her kisses. She loved him, he loved her, and they were apart because he'd been a stupid, arrogant ass.

He'd told himself she had to give him a second chance.

Really? a sly voice within him had whispered. *Just think of how you hurt her. She doesn't "have" to give you anything.*

By last night, he'd been close to crazy. He needed a plan. A logical plan. Logic was what had built him a fortune. Surely, it could win back a woman's heart.

And suddenly, late this afternoon, it had come

to him. A plan. Logical, imaginative, one that would surely work.

He'd headed straight for Tiffany's.

A gift a day. A heart a day. Diamonds, rubies, sapphires. Yellow gold. White gold. Platinum. All with notes saying he loved her. What woman would resist?

His Isabella. That was who.

The realization hit him as he looked at an exquisite array of jeweled hearts. Pendants. Earrings. Bracelets. Beautiful, all of them—but nothing like this would win Isabella.

Flowers, perhaps. Something simple and beautiful, flowers every day for a week, for a month...

Flowers? For a woman whose life was filled with them?

Rio had thanked the sales clerk. He said he'd look around a little more and he strolled slowly through the store, hoping some brilliant idea would come to him.

A couple was standing near a display case. Rio barely noticed them—but he overheard them.

"Someday," the man said softly, "someday, babe, I'll buy you everything in this case. I love you, you know. You—and our baby, growing inside you."

Our baby, growing inside you...

Rio damned near stopped breathing. He swung toward the couple. The man had his arm around his wife.

His very, very pregnant wife.

Dio! How could he have forgotten that night he'd made love to Isabella without a condom? For all he knew, she might be carrying his child.

Suddenly, there was no time to waste on plans. He knew exactly what he had to do.

A quick call to his lawyer to set things in motion. Within a couple of hours he had what he needed: the location of the bar he'd heard Dante and the rest of the Orsini brothers owned—and the fact that the brothers met there almost every Friday night.

This was a Friday night.

And now, he was here, facing her brothers and a man he figured had to be the formidable Anna's husband.

They looked as if they wanted to kill him.

He didn't blame them—but they couldn't kill him before he told them the truth. Part of the truth, anyway. He had no intention of telling them Isabella might be pregnant. That was too private, too special.

It was between the two of them.

"Well?" the one called Falco said. "You have something to say, say it. Then we'll beat the crap out of you."

Rio took a deep breath. "I'm in love with Isabella."

Four of them laughed. Not Dante, the man who had once been his friend. Dante simply narrowed his eyes.

"We're supposed to believe a lie told by a liar?"

Rio flushed.

"I lied about who I was. It was stupid but—"

The man called Nick said something vicious and moved forward. Dante put out a hand.

"Let him finish."

"But I thought it was harmless. I never intended to—to become involved with your sister."

"Involved," the one called Rafe said coldly.

All of the men had moved closer, as if to wall him in.

"That was what it was, at first," Rio said flatly.

"Then it changed. And I wanted to tell her the truth."

"Why didn't you?" Anna's husband said.

A muscle knotted in Rio's jaw.

"I would have," he said. "But I was afraid I'd lose her."

"You mean," Falco said, "you'd lose your innocent little toy."

"I mean," Rio said quietly, "I was afraid I'd lose the woman I'd fallen in love with."

"That's an interesting story," Falco said coldly. "Let's see if we have it straight. You wanted to take our sister to bed, so you told her a lie. Then you fell in love with her, so you went on with the lie."

Rio looked at Dante. "I was going to tell her that night you showed up. I asked you to give us a few minutes alone, remember?"

"And he didn't," Nick said. "Tough."

"He didn't, no. And then Isabella said some things—"

"Oh," Dante said with icy sarcasm, "and she hurt your feelings."

Rio flushed. "I'm not proud of it, of being so—

so goddamned pathetic that I let myself believe what my heart should have known wasn't true."

"Pathetic is right," Falco said. "If a man loves a woman he'd never believe lies about her."

"Not necessarily true," said Nick uncomfortably. He knew, all too well, how easy it was to be a dumb SOB who'd listen to his head instead of his heart.

Silence. Then Rafe said, "So, what now? Why are you here?"

"Yeah," Dante said. "If any of this is true, why are you here instead of at Izzy's?"

"I'm here," Rio said, "because I was born in Italy and I've lived my life in Brazil. Both cultures are my own—and there are still those Italians and Brazilians who think it proper to go to the family of the woman you love and tell them you are going to marry her."

For some reason, the Orsini brothers all looked at Draco Valenti, who nodded in a way that made it clear confronting the family of the woman you loved made a lot of sense to him.

"You sound very sure of yourself, D'Aquila."

"I am sure of the fact that I love Isabella and she loves me."

In any other circle, such male arrogance might have raised some eyebrows. In this bunch, it brought nods of the head.

"We love each other," Rio said. His voice took on an edge. "And all of you better get used to it."

Dante raised his eyebrows. So did the others.

"Well, well, well," he said softly. Then he stuck out his hand. "Go for it," he said.

Rio shook Dante's hand, then the hands of the others.

"I'm happy to have met you all," he said formally.

"Yeah," Falco said. "But if our Izzy kicks you out, you'll meet us again—and next time, you won't be so happy about it."

The six men grinned at each other, and then Rio hurried from the room.

Isabella sat on the sofa in her tiny living room, shoes kicked aside, bare feet up on the coffee table.

She was exhausted, but not from gardening.

She'd had to stop digging and kneeling and sweating in the sun. You couldn't do those things and then toss your cookies all over a client's toes, not if you wanted to keep those clients.

Besides, she'd had something more important to do today.

She'd bought half a dozen early morning pregnancy test kits on her way home from Anna's last night and finally found the courage to use them this morning.

The EPTs had made things worse.

Two said she wasn't pregnant, three said she was, and she'd been so nervous she'd dropped one in the toilet before she could pee on it. So she'd phoned her GYN's office and said she had to have an appointment, no, not in two weeks, not next week.

"Today," she'd said in the firm voice of the new Isabella. And then the old Izzy had added a very polite "please."

And she was still in the dark.

Her gynecologist said she might be pregnant. On the other hand, she might not be. The doctor was rushed, the lab was busy, and the upshot was that the earliest she'd have a definite answer was tomorrow or, more probably, Monday, because tomorrow was Saturday and, *really, Ms. Orsini, the lab only works half days on Saturday and then it's only for emergencies...*

Isabella groaned and put her head back against the couch.

A few days ago, she'd refused to consider pregnancy as a possibility. Denial had her convinced she had a summer virus. Even when she'd let herself think about pregnancy, she'd done nothing to find out the truth.

Now, she wasn't sure she could endure the next twenty-four or forty-eight or how many endless hours it would be until she knew.

She wanted to know, right now. She *had* to know; she had plans to make, whether to remain pregnant, assuming she really was, or to terminate it, or have the baby and give it up for adoption...

Except, she knew the answer.

She'd have her baby. Keep it. Nurture it. Love it, this life she and her lover had made together. Her lying lover...

Had he intended to tell her the truth? That was what he'd said, but—but, it didn't matter.

Matteo was history, and it was funny but now she thought of him as Rio, because that was who he really was. A strong, proud man who'd created an existence out of nothing.

It didn't matter what name she gave him.

They'd both lived a lie and now—now they were lost to each other, forever.

A sob burst from her throat.

"I love him," she whispered, "I'll always love him—"

Isabella's cell phone rang. She wiped her eyes with her hand and checked the screen. Anna. She'd call her back. She wasn't up to speaking with anybody right now, not while she was being such a fool, crying over a man who could have come after her if he'd really loved her, who shouldn't have believed her terrible lies except yes, he should have, that was why she'd told him those lies, so he *would* believe them—

Brring, brring, brring.

The doorbell. Of course. Anna had phoned while she was climbing the five flights to Isabella's flat. Now what? Answer the door? Not answer it? Leave Anna, and all her good intentions, in the hall?

Brring, brring, brring.

Isabella sighed, rose to her feet, went to the door. Such impatience was so typically Anna.

"Okay," she said wearily as she undid the lock, the chain, the dead bolt. "Can't you take a hint? Somebody doesn't answer the bell, somebody doesn't want visit—"

The words caught in her throat as the door swung open. It wasn't Anna standing in the hall. It was Matteo. It was Rio. It was the love of her life. Tall. Handsome.

And angry.

Angry? Isabella frowned. What did he have to be angry about?

She would have asked him but he caught her by the shoulders, gave her a little shake and said, "Damnit, Isabella—"

And then his mouth captured hers.

It wasn't what he'd planned.

He'd rehearsed his lines in the taxi, gone over and over what he was going to say. That he'd lied about his name but not about who he was and never about his feelings for her. That he loved her and she loved him and, damnit, she'd lied, too—

Reality had driven all that logical planning from his mind.

His Isabella lived in a neighborhood that could, at best, be described as diverse. Her building was decrepit. She had five flights of steps to climb.

He was ticked off by the time he reached her door. And when he heard her undoing all those locks, when he saw her looking pale and exhausted and thin, when all of those things happened, he grew so angry at himself for not having told her what a liar he was, for not having confessed his love, for not having carried her off and made her his bride weeks ago that the only thing he could do was kiss her.

That, at least, was logical.

So was the fact that after a few seconds of struggle, she wrapped her arms tightly around his neck, lifted herself against him and kissed him back.

It took all the determination he possessed to take his lips from hers.

"You are the love of my life," he said.

And he waited.

For the first time in more than a decade, Rio D'Aquila waited.

It seemed to take forever. Then, at last, Isabella smiled.

"And you are mine," she said.

Rio's heart, frozen solid as ice the past endless weeks, the past endless years, thawed at the sound of those sweet words.

"Isabella," he whispered against her mouth, and he followed her name with a string of words in Italian, in Portuguese, none of which she understood, but she didn't have to.

He loved her. Her lover loved her.

"Isabella, *mia bella* Isabella, forgive me. I loved you from the minute I saw you."

"I don't believe you," she said, her lips curving in a smile. "You'll have to keep kissing me until I do."

"I love you," he said huskily. "That's why I was so afraid to tell you the truth. I thought you would hate me—"

"I did," Isabella said, between kisses. "That's why I told you my own lies. Here's the truth. I love you. I'll always love you."

Rio grinned. "Say it again."

"I love you. I love you. I love—"

More kisses. Then Rio framed her face with his hands.

"Marry me, Isabella."

Her eyes glittered with happy tears. She smiled—and then her smile dimmed.

"Ask me on Monday."

"What?"

"By Monday—" She hesitated. Should she tell him the truth? Yes. Absolutely. She would never lie to him again. "By Monday, I'll know if—if I'm pregnant. You might feel differently if—"

"Trust me, sweetheart," Rio said, with a smile so sexy it made her breath catch. "If you're not pregnant now, I'll make you pregnant as soon as I can."

Isabella laughed. "You will, huh?"

"I want a tiny Isabella in our lives."

"It could be a tiny Rio. Or a Matteo… Which reminds me, what do I call you?"

Rio smiled.

"Call me your beloved," he said huskily, "as I will call you mine."

EPILOGUE

EVERYONE agreed that Isabella was the most beautiful bride in the world, just as her sister and her sisters-in-law had been before her.

She wore a floor-length gown of ivory lace, her mother's lace veil and an antique diamond tiara Anna had found in a tiny Greenwich Village shop.

"It just had your name on it," Anna explained when she pinned it carefully into Isabella's dark curls.

The sisters smiled, hugged each other…and wept.

There was, Rio noticed, a lot of weeping going on.

"It's what happens when you have six sisters at one wedding," Rafe said drily, but they all knew how lucky they were that Anna and Isabella, Gabriella and Elle, Alessia and Chiara felt as if they were sisters by blood, not only by marriage.

All of them were Isabella's bridesmaids, though Anna, of course, was her matron of honor.

Raffaele, Falco, Nicolo, Dante and Draco, handsome in their Armani formal wear, stood witness for Rio, equally handsome in his.

They all called him Rio; it was what Isabella called him because it was his legal name and it seemed to suit him better than the name the orphanage had bestowed upon him.

This time, the wedding planner—they'd used the same one for all the Orsini nuptials—knew there was no point telling them you couldn't have that many best men at the altar.

In fact, she said, with a little sigh, she'd decided that this was how things *should* be done, if only a groom and his friends looked like these.

After the ceremony at the little Greenwich Village church, limousines took them to the Orsini mansion. The enormous conservatory behind it had been decorated with baskets and baskets of flowers from Isabella's shop.

There was music and incredible food—Anna, experienced at this by now, had dealt with the catering. And there were endless bottles of vintage champagne, though, as in the past, the brothers—

or maybe, this time, it had been Draco—somebody, at any rate, managed to sneak in a few bottles of chilled beer.

Isabella drank only chilled Pellegrino.

She was pregnant, and she glowed as only a happily pregnant woman can glow.

The day was winding down. All the guests had left. Only the band and the family remained when Cesare Orsini stepped up to the microphone, tapped on his champagne flute, cleared his throat and announced he had something to say.

Everyone was surprised.

Their father—the don—had not made any kind of speech at any of the other weddings. He had, if anything, kept to the background, for which his sons and daughters had been grateful.

None of them had any illusions about what he was.

None except Sofia, Cesare's wife and their mother. It was for her that Rafe, Dante, Falco and Nick, Anna and Isabella maintained an illusion of peace with their father.

So when he commandeered the microphone, the Orsini offspring frowned at each other.

The brothers and brothers-in-law instinctively

offered their wives protection from whatever their father might say.

Rafe put his arm around Chiara; Dante did the same with Gaby. Falco took a stance behind Elle and wrapped his arms around her waist. Nick reached for Alessia's hand. Anna settled in the curve of Draco's arm, Isabella in the curve of Rio's.

The Orsini grandchildren—there were six of them by now—had long ago been put down for naps by their nannies.

Silence descended over the conservatory.

"This," Cesare said into the mike, "is a very happy day." He smiled and raised his champagne flute to Isabella and Rio. "Isabella, my daughter, your mama and I wish you and your new husband joy."

Isabella nodded. "Thank you," she said stiffly.

Cesare grinned slyly. "Can you imagine what might have happened if I had not told you that accepting a job as a landscaper was not the right thing for you to do, hmm?"

Isabella stared at her father. "What?"

"Ah, *i miei amati figli,* my beloved sons and

daughters, you have no idea how much you mean to me."

"He's right," Falco said, sotto voce, "we sure as hell don't."

"Shh," Elle said softly, but she turned her face up to his and smiled.

"And you have no idea how much I respect you," Cesare said. His voice wobbled and he cleared his throat. "None of you chose to follow in my footsteps, for which I am very, very grateful."

A murmur swept through the room.

"When I was a young man, I dreamed of having children who would make your mama and me proud. And you have done exactly that. We are proud of you all."

The murmur grew in intensity. Cesare cleared his throat again.

"You have chosen your professions and your mates wisely. You are happy, and that is what we wanted most in this sometimes ugly world." He turned to his wife and held out his hand. Sofia took it and stood beside him. He bent his head, whispered to her, and she smiled. "Your mama has something she wishes to say."

Cesare took her hand and lifted it to his lips,

which sent another murmur through the room. Sofia looked at her children and their spouses. Her eyes glittered with unshed tears. She looked, Isabella would say later, like a bride herself.

"Your papa has told you how much we love you," Sofia said softly. "How much we respect you for your choices." She paused and looked up at her husband. "My wish for you all is that you will love each other as much as your father and I."

This time, the murmur that went through the room was filled with amazement. Quiet, docile Mama, professing love for her crime boss husband?

Sofia put her hand on Cesare's arm.

"I know it is difficult for you to understand. I know what your father is, what he has had to become. I know it in ways you cannot possibly comprehend and while I deplore the life he had to choose, I love him with all my heart." She looked at each of her sons and daughters in turn. "And because we love each other, we hoped that you would all find love, too." She paused. "But we began to worry—*I*—began to worry that you would not."

Isabella stepped forward. "What are you talking about, Mama?"

"Cesare," Sofia said, "you tell them, *si?*"

Cesare Orsini put his arm around his wife's waist.

"Your mama was concerned. Our sons, she said, were too content with bachelorhood. Our daughters were even worse. One was sometimes arrogant and opinionated."

Anna blushed. They couldn't possibly mean her.

"The other was filled with quiet strength and courage, but unable to see her true self."

Now, it was Isabella who blushed. Her new husband smiled and drew her to him.

"So," Cesare said, "we looked around. We saw things. Heard things. We put our heads together. What kinds of situations would catch the interest of our sons? Our daughters? And then, we sent you on errands we hoped might change your lives."

The Orsinis looked at each other. No. It was too much to absorb. Their parents, their quiet mother and tough father, playing cupid?

"Could it be true?" Isabella whispered to Rio.

Rio gathered his wife into his arms.

"I found you, didn't I, *bella mia?* So, I would say, yes, when it comes to love, anything can be true."

"Le nostre benedizioni su di voi e ai vostri figli," Cesare said. "Our blessings on you and your children. And now, *per favore,* your mama and I would like to share the dance floor with you before this beautiful day ends."

The band began to play. The tune was soft and haunting.

Rio led his wife onto the dance floor. Draco did the same with Anna. Rafe, Dante, Falco and Nick followed with their wives until the entire Orsini clan, Cesare and Sofia included, was waltzing to the beautiful music.

It was Anna who caught on first.

"Ohmygod," she said to Draco, "it's the theme from *The Godfather!*"

Everyone heard her. They all began to laugh.

"Now," Isabella whispered to her bridegroom, and Rio grinned, swept his wife into his arms and carried her off into the night while his new family cheered.

* * * * *